I'm A DRAG Not A Fag

Women please understand me
Men, please don't judge me
God please forgive me

---

a novel

by

Antoinette Smith

STTP Books
Riverdale, GA

Published in the U.S.A. by Straight to the Point Books
Riverdale, Georgia

ISBN: 1-930231-43-1 / 978-1-930231-43-6

Editor: Windy Goodloe
Cover Design: Marion Designs
Interior Book Layout: The Rod Hollimon Company

Printed in the United States of America

Acknowledgements

I would like to, first and foremost, thank God for giving me the ability to write. Not only did He give me a gift and a talent, He also gave me the strength to speak up about my past and help others in pain as well. I strongly believe that God has a purpose for everyone's life.

I have to thank my Dream Team— Mr. Rod Hollimon, my publisher/friend; Ms. Windy Goodloe, my excellent editor/friend; and Mr. Keith Saunders, book cover designer.

I have to give thanks to my God-Mommy (Myola Smith) and my God-Daddy (Mr. Dennis Pete). I want to thank you two for the never-ending motivation that you give me and the unconditional love that I feel from you guys.

I would like to thank my fans for believing in me. I would like to also thank my fans for keeping me lifted, by letting me know that they are indeed looking forward to my next book.

I would like to give a special thanks to Ocean's 66 in College Park, Big Daddy's Catering, Wheels and Tires by Johnnie Bailey.

I would also like to give a special thanks to my Mexican family at El Ranchero Mexican restaurant in College Park. I will list all of their names because they are all very special to me, so here goes…

George, Robert, Nacho, Penguin, Cheo, Alicia, Luis, Juan Luis, Crilin, Chava, Elias a.k.a Fred Flintstone, Sulvador, Memo, Joaquin, Cesar, Gus, Paco, El Jaliskillo, Antonio a.k.a Harry Potter, Jackie Chan, Nasa, That Red Bitch, Tifany, a.k.a Girl Power, Daniel, Christian, Danielle & Maria(we miss you),

Beto, Chunga, Negro, Miguel, Chuto, Wicho, Hugo, Tito, Zorro, Gilles Saint-Germain, and Cacheton.

I would also like to thank Blue and his Dark Blue Security Team— Rico_Strong, Tee, Cedric Williams, and Tawan.

I would also like to thank the College Park Police Department.

I can't forget to give a special thanks to my baby Dee!!"

I have to say…if it wasn't for pain, I wouldn't be who I am today. Sometimes pain is good, so don't look at it as a bad thing.

To my kids, who are known as my 5 Lights, I write for you, for us— Pinky! Driah! Clyde! Chicken! Fat Boy!

I meant it when I said that I would write us out of the hood… I love you all so much!

You Only Need One Person to Believe in You and That's You!

Antoinette Smith

A Special Dedication

To My Loved Ones and Friends Who are Gone Too Soon and Most Definitely Never Forgotten…

Hattie Lee Reid Pearson
Oscar Pearson
Vurilyn Toon
Harry Pearson
Willie Pearson
Lucile Brown
Arthur Brown
Nelson "Hump" Redmon
Tremeesa "Rat" West
Yvonne "Sister" Walker
Claudette McGhee
Willie McGhee
Patricia Ann Walker
Sabrina "Shawn" Murphy
Carrie Mae Wilson
Kathy "Kitty Kat" Carter
Daryl Carter
Acie "Hubbard" Wilson
Pearline Strowder
Catherine "Dot Dee" Simpson
Robin Lynn Jones
Devorris "DMoss" Moss
Beth Nicole "Candygurl" Dodson
Omar "O" Jerrod Brown
Ronald Jerome Holston
Michael Jackson
Whitney Elizabeth "Nippy" Houston
Trayvon Martin

God picks special flowers,
and these are a few that He added to His Heavenly Garden.

The books that I write will hit close to home,
But someone had to turn the pain on.
Living with a lot of pain built up
Will do nothing but mess your life up.
You could have a wonderful family and think that you've
got it made,
And some of us will even take this pain to our grave.
It's okay to be ashamed, but GOD has a plan for us all.
We weren't put on this earth to walk perfect; we were
designed to fall,
And after that fall, all you have to do is get back up,
And make sure that there is nothing but faith in your cup.
There is a GOD because He made me see
That there is more to life than just worrying about me.
I will open doors for a lot of people,
Even if my novels never EVER have a sequel.
You can read my books and say,
"I, too, can write a book someday!"

Every soul has a story to tell.
If you can write a sentence, you can write a book.
Antoinette Smith

A Letter from the Author

No one on this green earth has the right to judge you because of your sexual preference. I wrote this book with so much passion, and I wrote it with several silenced hearts in mind. Don't be scared to come out of whatever shell that you're living in. God only gave you one precious life to live, and He doesn't want you to live it in distress. God wants us all to be happy, and, if being with the same sex make you happy, then so be it! I respect people who stand for what they believe in. This one is for you.

I hope you enjoy my Straight to the Point book about a boy named Trey who really thought that he was a girl trapped in a boy's body....

If you or someone you know is a victim of bullying, please contact 1(800) 668-6868. You do not have to suffer in silence. There are people who will help you.

From the Twisted Mind of a Gemini

All my life, I knew I wanted to be a girl,
But Daddy wasn't having that in his world.
He knew that I didn't want to play ball,
But he made me, and that was his final call.
I never wanted to sleep with a girl,
And, when I did, it made my stomach curl.
My sister was the one who should have been a man
Because she looked like her name should have been Stan.
My mother did all she could to protect me,
But Daddy would just not let me be.
My sister had always had my back,
Especially when the kids would tease me and go on the war
path.
I love all of them, especially my dad,
But he'll never accept me as a fag.
God opened up my eyes for me to see
That the only one I should make happy is me.

1
Laying Down the Rules

My mother always laid down the rules before she left my sister and me home alone.

She'd say, "Cynthia, you and Trey are not to have any company on the inside or the outside of this house."

This meant that we couldn't play with our friends until the weekend.

Our parents worked all the time. Our mother worked as an operator for the local phone company, and our daddy was a fireman for the city of Atlanta. He worked part time at the fire station, and he normally did all of the cooking. His best dishes were steamed ox tails and curry chicken. He could also fry goat meat to perfection.

Daddy was from Jamaica. His whole family was still there, but I didn't know anything about them because he refused to talk about them. As a matter of fact, he never talked to me, unless he was yelling at me. If I had to use one word to describe my daddy, that word would be mean. Daddy had been mean since I'd known him. Along with his accent, the other indication that my father was an islander was the way he wore his hair. My daddy was tall and dark-skinned, and he had long dreadlocks that stopped midway down his back.

My mother, who was as sweet as pie and very conservative, didn't even look like she would be caught dead with Daddy, let alone be married to him. Mama was petite and light skinned with big, almond-shaped eyes. She had long, black hair that flowed down her back, but you would never know it was that long because she always kept it in a neat bun. Needless to say, she and Daddy were total opposites, but they were in love and had been for the last twenty-five years. Even after reflecting on all their differences, I thought that they looked good together, considering that they had been together all my life. They had hooked up in college, where they had both been talented student athletes. She was a basketball player, and he was a football player. He had hurt his knee in college and had being trying to live his dreams through me ever since.

My parents had only had two kids. My sister Cynthia and me. Cynthia was two years older than me. I didn't get any looks from Daddy. I looked just like Mama. Hell! I looked like a girl, and, because of this, my sister Cynthia had to defend me at school just about every day. The other kids teased me and called me names like "gay blade", "fruit cup", and "sweet pants". They were so evil that they even gave me the nickname "fruity booty". Luckily, my sister Cynthia was a tom boy, so she didn't mind fighting my battles.

One time, I came home from school crying because the kids had been teasing me. I ran to the kitchen to get a butcher's knife, and Cynthia came in after me. She was the only one who could calm me down. She said, "Trey, look at me! Those kids are just jealous of you."

She took the knife out of my hand and got prepared to fight my battle the next day at school. Every time she got into a fight over me, she usually got suspended from school for three days. And our dad Raymond would say, "Boy, you better put some bass in your voice and fight back. It's bad enough that you're walking around here looking and twisting like a damn girl. Your mama needs to cut that damn ponytail off, and then maybe you'll start acting like a damn man."

Daddy wanted to live his dreams through me. Since

he couldn't go pro in football, he wanted me to pursue his dream, but I wasn't hearing that shit. I had plans of my own. I didn't want to follow in his footsteps. I didn't want to walk in his shoes. I wanted to walk in some heels *alright,* and they were stilettos.

When Raymond talked down to me, my mother would always jump in and say, "Leave Trey alone. He's not a fighter."

My daddy would then say, "Carolyn, stop taking up for him and let him be a man. He needs to be a man!"

I knew Daddy was pissed off because he usually would have called Mama *baby* and not by her name. I hated that they were divided because of me. I hated that I was the reason they had heated arguments, but, no matter what, Daddy stayed there, and he never ran out on Mama, and there was a small part of me that really respected him for that.

When Cynthia and I were at home alone, we'd play school, dress up, and sing. I had wanted to be a teacher, but I knew I was going to be famous one day. And the only famous principal that I knew was Mr. Clark from the movie *Lean on Me.*

When we played school, Cynthia would be the teacher known as Ms. Burns, and I would be the student Trey Burns. When we played dress up, I would put on Mama's lingerie and a pair of her heels. I always looked so pretty. My hair was as long as hers, and it was black and silky, and I often wore it in a ponytail. And I had to give it to myself. I could sing if I couldn't do anything else. It seemed like Mama would always come home and catch me in her make-up and clothing. Mama knew that I was the one who played in her make-up, but she would punish Cynthia instead. I would tell a lie with a straight face, I would say that it was Cynthia who had been in it. And Mama knew that I was lying because

I never remembered to wipe off her lipstick from my face.

I told Mama over and over that I wanted to be a singer. I never wanted to play sports, but Raymond put me on the little league football team anyway. I never scored any touchdowns. I would watch the ball come my way, and I would just let it land on the ground. I knew the fundamentals of football, but I wanted to get my nails done instead of catching a fucking ball.

I played football up until the tenth grade. During one of our most important games, the coach called me and told me to go in.

He said, "Your team really needs you."

And he was right. I was really fast. I was the team's secret weapon, and I knew, if I went in, we would definitely win the game. I could have scored and made the winning points, but I refused to go in because it was a nasty, rainy day, so I sat on the sidelines and used a stick to draw in the mud.

The coach, who I knew wanted to ring my neck, yelled, "You need to take your punk ass home and sign up for cheerleading."

When he heard about this, my daddy was so mad at me that he took his frustrations out on the coach. My daddy took off his Jamaican hat and punched the coach in his face, but, to be honest, the coach was right— I should have been somewhere cheering. It looked like more fun anyway.

When we got home, Daddy gave me a good ass whipping. I can't recall how many ass whippings I got from Daddy. I had lost count, but that one in particular was one that I would never forget.

Cynthia would always cheer me up by coming into my room and playing dress up with me. She would sneak and bring me Mama's makeup, and I would forget all about

Daddy's hard hands.

Cynthia was the one who looked like a boy. She was the one outside playing flag football, while I was in the house listening to the radio and dancing in the mirror. She was the one with the muscles, and I wasn't. No one would ever tease her because she kicked butts, and she didn't take any shit from anyone. She was the one who had beat up Big Steve, the school's bully, numerous times while I watched.

One day, Big Steve punched me in my stomach and pulled my rubber band out of my hair. I came home and told Cynthia, and she threw fire ants all over him. He never messed with me again after that, but that still didn't stop the other kids from teasing me. When they teased me in places like the cafeteria, some of the teachers would get a few laughs in, too.

Cynthia used to tell me, "Boy, stop crying. They talked about Jesus Christ!"

I knew she wished that Mama would have just cut my damn hair off. I knew that she got tired of fighting my battles. Even though she didn't win them all, she won a majority of them. When I saw the teachers laughing at me, I knew that I had to come up with a plan for the whole school to think I was all man. I needed everyone to believe that I was not a "gay blade". I was going to prove myself, and I knew just how to do it.

2

I Fucked a Girl...YUCK

When I went into Cynthia's room, I found her lying across the bed doing a word find puzzle.

"Cyn-thia! Oh, Cyn-thia!"

She knew, whenever I called her name like, that I wanted something.

"Who do you want me to beat up now?"

"No one," I said as I sat on the edge of her bed. "I want you to record me fucking Trish."

"Crazy Trish from next door?"

"Yes. Cynthia, I have to prove to everyone at school that I am not a gay blade. I have to do something because I am tired of the whole school ridiculing me."

Trish lived next door to us, and she was a high school drop-out. She lived with her mother who was hardly ever home. For years, I had witnessed her sneaking boys in and out of her bedroom window.

"So, what's the plan?" she asked as she sat up in her bed. "And why do you want to fuck her out of all the girls you know?"

"Because she's right next door, and you could easily record us."

"Boy, you are still a virgin. Do you even know how to have sex?"

"Do you?" I asked as I reflected on her and Jayson having sex numerous of times.

We weren't supposed to have company, but, as long

as I got to play in Mama's make-up and heels, I didn't care that she snuck Jayson in. I didn't snitch on her, and she didn't snitch on me. We were so close, and I was glad that she had my back like that. She had been with Jayson ever since middle school. They were inseparable.

I looked at her and said, "All I have to do is stick my dick in her pussy and hunch. How hard is that?"

"Fool! Sex is more than hunching. You have to protect your dick from infectious diseases. There are diseases out here that will make your dick fall off!" She threw me a condom and told me to take my pants off. "First, you have to get your dick hard," she said as she closed the door.

"How do I do that?" I asked as I took my pants off.

"This will help," she said as she put a flick into the DVD player.

After watching the flick for some time, my dick began to grow.

She tore the condom open with her mouth and said, "Put it on this way with the tip facing outwards. When you cum, the condom will catch your sperm."

I was in the eighth grade. I didn't know anything about fucking. All I knew was Gladys Knight and Betty Wright's oldies.

"All you have to do is stroke your dick, and then you'll get a good feeling, and, when you get that feeling, you will ejaculate in the condom. Aren't you getting turned on by that lady's big breasts?"

She was more excited for me to have sex for the first time than I was. Her eyes had grown bigger and bigger as she talked.

"Your dick is big like Jayson's," she said before she turned to leave.

She bumped into the door as she left.

"Don't forget to pull the tip of the condom, so the sperm won't come out and make a mess."

I did what she said. I looked at my dick, then back at the flick. I thought, *I've never had sperm to come out of my dick before*. I put a firm grip around my dick. I began to jack it slowly, but, for some reason, when the lady was riding the man's dick, I didn't feel anything, but, when he turned her over and started fucking her from the back, I enjoyed watching the muscles in his back. I enjoyed watching his sexy-ass booty go in and out. I loved watching his thick eyebrows go up and down, and his six pack was to die for. He looked like Omari Hardwick.

I admired the man's muscles in his back as I watched him stroke back and forth. He pulled his dick out and started jacking it real fast, and so did I. We came at the same time. He skeeted on her ass, and, when I looked at the condom, it was filled to capacity. I let out a sigh of relief because I had just experienced the best feeling in the world. I looked at the man's face on TV, and I could tell that we were sharing that same feeling. I stood there, waiting for Cynthia to come back in. I was weak at the knees, but I really liked that feeling.

"That was fast," Cynthia said as she rolled some toilet tissue off the roll.

"What now?" I asked as I stood there, still high off of that wonderful sensation.

"Be still," she said as she put the tissue around my dick and rolled the condom off. "So, how did it feel to have an orgasm?" she asked as she threw the condom in the trash.

"That was the best feeling in the world," I said as I pulled my pants back up.

"All we have to do now is follow the plan accordingly. You just have to make sure you put on a condom because you know how Trish rolls."

"I will. You just make sure you come in and record us. I will make sure that I leave the front door unlocked."

When she left, I laid back on my bed and thought of Omari Hardwick.

The following day, I knocked on Trish's door. She came to the door, wearing only a T-shirt. *This girl stay ready,* I thought.

"What do you want?" she asked, looking me over from my head to my toe.

"I want to come and kick it with you."

She didn't protest as I walked in. I knew, then and there, that she was a straight up freak. I mean, the epitome of a freak. Her mother was never at home, and I knew that I had a chance to fuck her because she was the neighborhood whore. Trish had a caramel complexion and deep dimples in her chubby cheeks. She was very pretty, and I never really understood why she was the way that she was. She favored Shar Jackson from *Moesha*.

"So, what do you really want?" she said as she sat down on the couch with her legs wide open. "Do you want your hair braided or something?"

I looked at her and said, "I am a virgin, and I want you to be my first."

"Boy! Are you crazy? This pussy isn't free! What the fuck do I look like to you? I'm sure you know by now that this is what I do. Come on back to my room. Let me show you something."

And sure enough, when we got to her room, she had a list of her services taped on the wall. She charged for everything from hand jobs to fucking her in the butt. I couldn't believe my eyes.

"My mother is in jail, and somebody has got to pay the bills around here."

She was dead-ass serious. As I observed her prices, I saw that she charged one hundred dollars to get fucked in the ass. *Gross*, I thought as I looked straight at the bottom of the list. She charged fifty dollars to get fucked from the back. She charged two hundred dollars to do everything. That explained the nonstop traffic.

"Wow!" I said as I continued to look at the list. "You charge thirty dollars for someone to stick their fingers in your ass?"

"That's just for one finger. They have to pay sixty to stick two in my ass."

"So, how much money do you got?"

"I don't have any money."

"Well, you better go get some from your mama or daddy! You got to pay to play," she said as she lit an incense.

"Can you please just do this for me this one time?" I asked as I nibbled on my nails. *I was nervous as hell.*

"I guess I could make an exception because you are a pretty-ass boy. I don't know why, but, for some reason, I thought that you were gay," she said as she turned on the ceiling fan. "You'd make a pretty bitch," she said as she ran her fingers through my long, silky black hair.

"I am not gay," I said as I remembered that I had to go and unlock the door for Cynthia. "Have you ever fucked a dick this big?" I asked as I dropped my pants.

Her eyes looked like they were about to pop out of her head as she came closer.

"Your dick is so damn pretty," she said as she wrapped her hands around it with a kung fu grip. "This one will be on me," she said as she got down on her knees and prepared to suck my dick.

She put my whole dick in her mouth, balls and all, and she didn't gag or nothing. She sucked my dick like she was a professional prostitute. I guess she was, since she had a damn price list. Even I was enjoying her slurping and slobbing on my dick, I knew that this was what Cynthia needed to be recording. When I looked at the window, I saw Cynthia with the camcorder. I threw two thumbs up and pulled Trish's hair back while she sucked my dick like a pro.

"How does that feel?" she asked as she licked up and down my shaft.

"It feels good," I said as I tried to hold back my orgasm. I didn't want to cum in her mouth. I wanted to cum in her pussy.

"Are you ready to feel this pussy?" she asked as she pushed me back on the bed. She jumped on my dick so quick that I didn't have time to even think about putting on a condom. She was quick like lightning. Cynthia's voice popped in my head, but it was too late. Suddenly, I felt her sticky pussy juice running down my balls. I felt sick to my stomach. She rode my dick like she was in a rodeo contest. I had to make it look like I was enjoying it for the video, so I licked her nipples.

She moaned, "Suck them harder," as she rode my dick up and down.

I sucked on them, and they tasted salty. I felt like I was about to cum, but the feeling suddenly went away. Trish was screaming my name as she fucked me like a mad man. Then, I remembered the man in the video. I turned her over on her stomach and fucked her from the back. I imagined the man's dick from the video, and the more I thought about the hard veins in his dick, the closer I got to my peak. I thought about his six pack and all the muscles in his back that moved as he fucked the girl in the video. I thought about his thick eyebrows, and I imagined that it was him that I was fucking and not Trish. I closed my eyes and fucked her hard. Finally,

I exploded in her wet, sticky pussy. When it was all over, I felt like I had been violated. I hadn't enjoyed that one bit, but I was relieved that Cynthia had it all on video.

Trish grinned and said, "You can fuck me for free anytime. I love big dicks."

No fucking thanks. I never wanted to feel that gushy shit again, I thought as I put my hair back in a ponytail. When I went back home, Cynthia was watching the video.

"Trey, you didn't put the condom on like I told you to."

"So what! Did you get it all on video?"

"Trey, your sperm went in her. You could get her pregnant!"

"It's now or never for me to prove myself at school. I am tired of being the talk at the school," I said as I looked at myself on the video.

"You better pray that she don't have any diseases, or you will be the talk of the town."

"Who's the man now?" I said as I pointed at the TV.

"Look at how I'm hitting that pussy from the back!"

Cynthia knew the real me. She knew that I didn't want to fuck a girl. She knew, deep down inside, that I wanted to be a girl. She knew my darkest secrets. So, what if I fucked a girl? I still wanted to dress up and wear lipstick.

3
Raymond's Last Beating

I went to school and showed off the video to all the other kids. They were shocked, but I still felt deep down inside that I couldn't fool them. I felt like they didn't believe that I liked girls. The teachers had heard about the video, too, but they didn't entertain it. They knew that I walked with a twist, and, as I got older, I looked more and more like a girl, but the video did help put an end to a lot of the teasing. They didn't tease me as much in our senior year. Since it was my last year of high school, I decided to play on the football team. I planned to go to college once I graduated. The least I could do was play football for Raymond. Jayson was the quarterback. I made the whole team and the coach proud of me when I scored the winning touchdown at one of our most important games. They all picked me up and threw me around in the air. I enjoyed being thrown around by all those boys. It was the end of the school year, and Raymond hadn't changed one bit. He was still telling me to cut my hair. I didn't want to cut my hair, and I didn't want to play sports in college. I wanted to go to college to become a fashion stylist.

One night, Raymond and I got into a heated argument. I was well on my way to being a grown diva, and I didn't want to hear his mouth anymore about my future. He kept on saying that I was going to play college football. And finally I stood up and said, "Everyone isn't built for that football shit!"

Then, I ran into my room and slammed the door. I

knew that a beating was coming afterwards because I had never gotten that mad or had the nerve to curse at Raymond. I locked my door and sat at my computer. I looked up the term *faggot,* and it clearly stated that it was 'a guy who took nuts across the face'. I hadn't had that done to me, so, technically, I wasn't a faggot. Just because I had had sexual fantasies about men didn't mean I would have nuts across my face.

As I read this, Raymond beat on the door. Before I could get up to unlock the door, he kicked it down. And Mama was right behind him, but it was too late. He was on my ass like flies on shit. He threw me on the bed and wailed on my head, saying, "Ain't no son of mine going to be a damn faggot!"

"That's enough, Raymond!" My mama screamed at the top of her lungs, trying to get him off of me, but he was in a rage.

By this time, Cynthia had moved out with Jayson, and I wished that she was there to get him off of my ass, too, but there was no stopping him. He was literally trying to pull my hair out of my scalp. After about thirty minutes or so, he was, finally, tired of kicking my ass. He stopped and left my room. I was balled up on my bed, putting my hair back in place. Mama was crying and hugging me. She assured me that he was just mad that he had hurt himself in college.

"Well, what does that have to do with me, Mama? I don't want to play football. Look at me. I am as pretty as can be," I said as snot came out of my nose. I was crying so hard that I couldn't stop. "I played little league for him, and I played in middle school. Mama, I even played for him my senior year. What is this infatuation that he has with football?"

My mother wiped the tears that were rolling down my cheeks and said, "Your father loves you. He really does.

He just wants his one and only son to follow in his footsteps. Trey, I can't explain what goes on in your father's head, but I do know that he has love for you. When I was pregnant with you, he was so happy that I was having a boy. You were born with a head full of black hair. You were every bit of nine pounds, and Raymond just knew that you were going to play sports."

I continued to cry because, if that was love that Raymond was showing me, I didn't want it. I wanted to go to college to be a fashion stylist or a hair stylist. I had been voted best dressed at school, and I just knew that I would be dressing famous people one day.

"Trey, you can be whoever or whatever you want to be. You have all of my support. And I mean that with every drop of life that I have in my body. Trey, I love you with all of my heart, and I want to see you make it in life. I want you to be a successful business man."

"That's just it, Mama. I don't want to be a man—period. I want to be a famous drag queen. That doesn't mean that I will be a faggot. Mama, you know how I love to dress up and sing. You have witnessed this my whole life."

She looked at me and didn't say a word. Then, I saw tears roll down her face.

"Mama, please don't cry. Just be happy for me. I have a dream, and my dream is to go to California and become the world's most famous drag queen. Take RuPaul, for example. He's beautiful in drag, and he's a successful businessman, also."

I walked Mama over to my computer and pulled up pictures of RuPaul. She said, "He's very pretty."

"I know, Mama, and this could be your son. This could be me!"

She looked at him and said, "I bet his mother is proud

of him, too. So go for it!"

She hugged me so tight.

"Mama, I have been following his career, and he made it big, and so can I. Mama, I only need one person to believe in me, and that's me."

"Make that two," she said as she looked at my door that was off the hinges. She shook her head and said, "After your father cools off, he will fix your door."

"There is also going to be a slight delay in the college. I actually have a job lined up at a hair salon already. I went in there one day, and the owner, whose name is Mikkos "The Hair Doctor" Bolton, but, who insisted that I call her Peaches, said that I could come and work for her once I am of age. Mama, you are getting up in age, and I want to take care of you. Raymond might flip out and leave you. Who knows? That man is crazy! Mama, I really feel deep down inside that Raymond really hates me. I can't recall one time when I've actually heard him tell me that he loves me. Mama, you have always told me that you loved me, but not Raymond. He was too busy, trying to make me catch a damn football."

"I know, sweetheart," Mama said as she came closer and hugged me.

Raymond walked into my room and calmly said, "You got until the morning to get out of my house, you faggot."

He looked at the door on the floor and shook his head before he walked out. I looked at Mama and assured her that I would be just fine. I was only eighteen at the time, and my high school teacher knew about Daddy and his beatings. He said that I was always welcomed at his house.

The next day, I grabbed as many clothes as I could and packed them into my gym bag. Mama was cooking breakfast, and Raymond had already left for work.

"Come on in here and eat some food."

I sat my gym bag next to me on the floor. She looked at me and said, "Trey, your daddy didn't mean what he said last night. You are my son, and you do not have to leave this house."

"Mama, it's only going to make things worse if I stay. I'll be fine, and I will make sure to call you every day. I have dreams to fulfill. I don't want you to bury me because Raymond did say that he would kill me dead."

"Well, before you leave I have something to give you." She went to her bedroom and came back with a white envelope. "Here. This should help, while you're out there. Trey, those streets are mean, and people shouldn't hate and judge, but some people hate gay people."

"Mama, technically, I am not gay. I plan on being a famous drag queen. And that's a big *if* on whether I get my sex changed or not, then I wouldn't be gay. I would be all woman."

She sat down in the chair and put her hand over her head.

"Mama, I'm just speaking hypothetically. Look at me. What else could I be in life? I have hair that's down to my back. My face could be on the cover of *Vogue*. My cheekbones are so high that when I smile you can barely see my eyes. My waist is a size three. And I wear a size seven in shoes. I am better than your average woman. Don't you see that I am meant to be the world's next famous drag queen?"

"Trey, just be careful and know that I love you with all of my heart."

I knew right then and there that Mama would accept me as a woman. She would just have to accept the fact that she had two daughters now.

After I ate my breakfast, I counted the money that she'd given me.

"Mama, this is a lot of money. Where did you get this from? Did you rob a bank or something?"

"No, Trey. I had it set aside for a rainy day."

"More like a tsunami," I said as I snapped my fingers.

I shocked myself when I did that snap. She didn't say anything about the snap, but I knew she was probably thinking that I had it bad.

I had my mama's stamp of approval, so I was now ready to go out and take on the world. I grabbed my gym bags and headed for the door. She grabbed me again, hugged me real tight, and said, "Trey, I love you no matter what you become in life. Just don't become dead."

Then, she kissed me on both of my cheeks.

"I promise I will call you every day. You have my word," I said as I headed to the front door.

4
Tricks are for Kids

I caught the bus to Mr. Peyton's house. He lived on the West Side, in the Cascade area. I really hoped that he would be just as glad to see me as I would be to see him. I didn't have anywhere else to go. Going to live with Cynthia and Jayson was completely out of the question. She had started a new job as an accountant downtown, and Jayson was spoiled rotten. He was one of those kids who would live off of his parents forever.

As I sat on the bus, I sat my gym bag next to me on the seat instead of the floor. I didn't want anybody to sit with me. Some people that rode public transportation did not know the meaning of hot water and soap.

When Cynthia and I used to catch the downtown bus to Underground Atlanta, when I was just a kid, sometimes, the buses were so crowded that I had no control over who sat by me. Sometimes, Cynthia would have to find a seat in the back. It was just that crazy. So, now that I was older, I refused to sit by a funky-ass bus rider. I laid my head back and reminisced. I thought about how my teacher first told me that no one had accepted him when he came out of the closet. He knew that I was having problems at home, and there were plenty of times I had cried on his shoulder. He was such a good teacher and friend. He told me that his mother had found out through an aunt who he thought was trustworthy enough to keep his secret. Turns out, his auntie couldn't hold water. He said that she was like an old refrigerator— she was always somewhere running her mouth. And, sure enough, during his second semester in college, his mother kicked him out, so I knew that he would understand my pain.

After an hour long ride, I got off the bus and walked to his community. I didn't have a code to the security gate, so, when a car came by, I ran through the gate.

His community was so nice. His house was worth well over six hundred thousand. Once I got to the door, I rang the doorbell a few times. When there was no answer, I knocked hard on his iron entry doors. After a few more minutes, he answered the door, while throwing his dreads out of his face.

"Trey, what are you doing here?" he asked as he opened the door. Then, he looked at my face and said, "Oh, my God! Did your father do this to you?"

"Yes, he beat me, and he put me out, and that was it. There's no going back. I have nowhere else to go. You've always told me that your home is my home. Does that offer still stand?"

"Sure! Come on in, and let me get you something to drink."

I looked around his house and saw that he had done well for himself. I knew the school system didn't pay him that much, but he had made the best of it. He had everything from Natuzzi Italian leather sofas to paintings on the wall by Georgia O'Keefe. I was impressed by how clean and neat his place was. He was living like a millionaire.

As I looked around the house, he disappeared. While I was admiring one of his O'Keefe painting, he came back with a bottle of spring water.

"Why are you looking like that?" he asked. "Were you expecting a stiff drink or something?"

"No, I am amazed at how nice your place is. The last

time I was over here, you only had a sofa bed, and now you have pretty silver sterns in every corner, and you have this nice, thick turtle design Tabriz rug in the middle of the floor. This is how I want to live when I move to California. Mr. Peyton, my eye doesn't feel as bad as it looks. I have a terrible headache from last night, though. My daddy was trying to pull my hair out of my scalp. You should have seen him. He was a worse than a mad Russian."

"Well, you're safe here, and you can live here as long as you'd like," he said as he gave me two aspirins. "Remember, I was once in your shoes, so I know exactly what you're going through. And, Trey, I'm not your teacher anymore, so you can call me Ronnie. Come on. Let me show you to your bedroom."

He led me through the foyer to the back of his house. "You can use this computer, and you have access to all the cable channels. Just put it like this. *Mi casa es su casa.*"

He hugged me. I jumped on the pillow top bed and said, "This feels just how it looks."

That night, Ronnie and I had a ball. We watched movies and talked about old times in school. After he went to his bedroom, I sat in my new bed and thought about my future. *What do I really want to be? Will I be accepted in the world? Will I ever become the victim of a hate crime like Mama said?* There were so many questions running through my head that I didn't know what to do. I knew that I wanted to be known for something. I wanted to be a famous designer. If Gianni Versace could do it, then so could I. He was human, just like I me. He didn't have any special powers; he only had a powerful imagination.

Just before I was fell sound asleep, all of a sudden, I heard Ronnie say, "It's not what it looks like! He was a student of mine, and he needs a place to stay!"

I could tell that he was pleading with another man. They both were standing in my room arguing over me. I sat up in the bed and wiped my eyes to get a clearer view. Before I could say a word, the short white man came over to me and put a gun to my head.

"Chris, calm down! This is only a student! Don't do this," Ronnie pleaded with Chris. "We didn't have sex or anything. I promise! Chris, please put the gun down! This friendship is platonic. I swear to you."

My life flashed before my eyes ten times, and the only vision that gave me any comfort was RuPaul in drag.

The whole time, Chris just stood there, with a revolver at my temple.

"Chris, you were supposed to be out of town, so why are you home so early?" Ronnie asked.

"I'm glad I came home and caught you red-handed. So, what do you have to say for yourself, Mr. Cheater? Get your ass out of this bed," he said as he pulled back the thick, fluffy black comforter. "Get up, you fucking, young-ass faggot!"

"You're a faggot, too" I said, without thinking that he could pull the trigger and end my life in a blink of an eye. I stood up, revealing my fully erect penis. I didn't know why it was hard; it just was.

"I see why you're cheating on me. This little motherfucker is packing! Here I am, going all across the world for you to get a bigger dick, so our love life can be complete. I know that God didn't bless me with a big dick, but you married me for better or for worse."

I was standing there, praying to God that my dick would go down, but it never did. It stood straight up at attention.

"Chris, I love you, and I never meant for any of this

to happen. We had a few drinks, and then one thing led to another."

I didn't recall us having anything to drink that night. All we did was watch movies and talk about the old school days.

"Yeah! That's what you said when I caught you with that other student."

"Shhh...Please don't say his name," Ronnie demanded.

"His name is Jayson."

"White boy Jayson? My sister's boyfriend?" I said in disbelief.

I have always had a crush on him, ever since I first saw him naked in the locker room when we played football together at school, I thought as I stood there, looking like a fool.

"May I please put on my clothes?" I asked as chill bumps grew all over my body.

"No, you can't!" he screamed. "You can go over there and let Ronnie fuck you in your pretty little ass. No never mind that. I have a better idea. Why don't you suck his dick like you're eating a piece of chicken 'cause I know how y'all niggers love some fried chicken."

"But I've never —"

He cut me off. As I walked over to Ronnie, he cracked a smile. I didn't find anything funny. Chris pulled the trigger and out came the word BANG.

"Who is this?" I asked as my heart began to beat at its normal rhythm.

"Trey, this is Chris, my lover, and we thought that we'd have a little fun with you."

Chris walked over and hugged me and said, "You were scared as hell."

I let out a deep breath and said, "You have no idea. I

thought you was going to kill me."

"I know that Ronnie would never cheat on me. He's been my partner since college. You were sleeping so good, so we decided to play a prank."

"Now, can I put my pants back on?" I asked as I walked to get my jeans off of the floor.

"Sure. We were just goofing around," Chris said.

"Trey, I would like to formally introduce you to the Chris "the Rainbow" Hyatt. He is a fashion designer, and, from what you told me last night, he could be the ticket to your success. He could give you some tips before you just up and run to California. It's stupid to think that your dreams will just happen overnight."

5
Living It Up

I really enjoyed living it up with Ronnie and Chris. They didn't rush me to do anything as far as getting a job or continuing my education. Plus, I had plenty of Mama's money left. Mama had given me five thousand dollars. The only time I spent any money was when I had to buy personal items such as deodorant and oil sheen for my long, black silky hair. Chris had given me his American Express card, but I could never quite use it in the fashion that I wanted to use it in. I mean, I was the child that they never had. They were so overprotective of me. Even though I told them that I would be getting a job at Peaches' Hair Salon soon, they took care of me and told me that I owed them nothing.

Peaches was a cool chick. I had met her the day after Raymond had whipped my ass for not catching the ball at football practice. There was no use in fighting back because my nails were long, and I didn't want to break them. Besides, if I had raised one hand at Raymond, I would have been dead. He would always say, "I brought your faggot ass into this world, and I don't have a problem with taking your faggot ass out."

I ran out the house and jumped on the MARTA bus. I didn't know where I was going. Finally, I rang the bell and got off in Downtown Atlanta. Peaches' salon caught my attention as soon as I got off of the bus. It was lit up with the words THE HAIR DOCTOR in neon colors. As I walked in, I saw seven stations. Square mirrors covered the walls throughout. She had a long, purple carpet in the middle of the floor. *I would look good walking that runway,* I thought.

She immediately said, "How can I help you?"

I was still teary eyed, but I looked her in her eyes and said, "Can I have a job please?"

She cracked a smile and said, "Son, you're too young to work here. How old are you anyway?"

As we talked, she swept up the hair that lay on the floor.

"I am seventeen. And I can do a lot of stuff, like shampoo hair. I can wrap hair, and I can glue tracks in, too."

"Hold on a second. Your mouth is moving fifty miles per hour."

I observed her big, beautiful eyes as she put me in my place. She was a little shorter than me, and she was brown skinned. She had on a graffiti style apron. Her hair was long and curly, and it was almost to her ass. Her eyes were to die for. The eye shadow that she had on matched her apron. Her eyes were the first thing that I noticed because she had on a pair of the longest eye lashes that I had ever seen. I knew I was a blabber mouth as soon as I walked in. She was closing, and it was just me and her in there, so I figured that I could just talk to her. She seemed like a very understanding person. I sat in a chair and grabbed one of her books that had her styles in it. She could lay some hair. I mean she had styles in there from real short hair all the way to hair almost to the floor. I could tell why she called herself the Hair Doctor. She could really doctor on her clients' heads.

She looked at my hair. Then, she walked over and touched it. She said, "What kind of hair is this?"

I snapped, "Mine! What kind of hair is in your head?"

"This is Indian hair," she said as she pulled a strand for me to feel. And it felt like Indian hair, too. It was silky and soft, just like mine. We both laughed, and we were cool ever since. She explained to me that I was too young to work in her shop, but she did promise me a job once I turned eighteen. I got her business card, and, from that day on, we talked on the phone often. I thought she was so sweet to talk to me when I needed someone to talk to. She didn't bite her tongue for shit. She let me know when I was wrong, and she let me know when I was right, but, according to me, I was always right and never wrong.

After reminiscing about Peaches, I decided to go upstairs and see what Ronnie and Chris were up to. As I was about to knock on their bedroom door, I noticed that it was cracked, and I heard noises. My ears weren't deceiving me, and my eyes confirmed what my ears were hearing. I put my head in the crack and watched as Ronnie fucked Chris in his ass like there was nothing to it. Chris's short blonde bob was sweaty, and Ronnie's dreads were going everywhere. They were fucking like two wild animals in the jungle. I had got a hard-on just standing there watching the two of them. I mean, my dick had gotten rock hard. Before I knew it, I had unzipped my pants and was stroking my dick. I was stroking it in rhythm to the movements of Ronnie's back. When he fucked Chris slow, I stroked my dick slow, and, when he fucked Chris fast, I stroked my dick fast.

Chris kept saying, "Yeah, daddy! Fuck me just like that! I can take it! Put all of daddy's dick in my white ass!"

Ronnie, while he fucked him, slapped him on his ass, turning it pink. I was stroking my dick so fast until, finally, sperm shot out of my dick like a rocket. It was a good thing that the bathroom was right down the hallway. I went in there and cleaned myself up and got my sperm up off the wall. Afterwards, I went to my room and thought about how easy Ronnie's dick looked going in and out of Chris's ass. It didn't look painful at all. Maybe, it was time for me to get fucked in my ass, too, but by who?

6
So Long Daddy

It had been a while since I had talked to Cynthia. I knew her and Jayson were living it up in Buckhead. I wondered if I should tell her that Jayson was on the down low. Chris did say that Ronnie had fucked him when they played that prank on me. I didn't know if he was playing or not, but I was going to find out on my own. I had kind of suspected that he was a little on the sweet side because, one day, in the locker room after a football game, I had popped him on his behind with a towel, and he said, "Boy, if you were a girl, then maybe."

He didn't get pissed or anything, so I kind of took that as a green light.

Not long after I had moved into Ronnie's, Mama called me and told me that Daddy had left her because I was going off to live my life as a fag and not as a football player. She went on talking about how he had wanted his only son to walk in his shoes and be a football player. The only shoes I wanted to walk in were a pair of Christian Louboutins. Fuck a pair of cleats! But I heard the pain in Mama's voice, and I asked her if she needed the money back that she had given me. She told me no. She said that, a few days earlier, she had been lucky enough to hit the lottery. She had hit the jackpot for a little over fifty million dollars. I was happy that she had plenty of money, but I was sad because she loved Daddy, and he was the only man that she'd ever known. They'd been together since college. She was fifty-five, and Daddy was fifty-nine. I was so scared of Daddy that the thought of me trying to set Mama up with another man was out of the question. Daddy would have wrung my neck out, and I knew that he would. I tried to change the subject and get Mama's mind off of Daddy, so I said, "Since you've hit the lottery, you can move to a better side of town."

She didn't want to move because she and Daddy had been in that house for more than twenty years, so I said, "But just think, you can finally get that country kitchen that you've always talked about."

"Well, I guess I could," she said as cried into the phone.

"Mama, don't cry. You'll be just fine. I'm sorry I couldn't be what you guys wanted me to be, but I have a life of my own, and football is out of the question."

"I know, son, but you know how your father is. You're his only male seed."

I had never disrespected Mama, but I was about to let her have a piece of my mind if she said one more thing about football. Luckily, she changed the subject and said that she had been looking at some houses north of Atlanta. We lived on the Southside in Lovejoy. Our house was a tri-level with four bedrooms. *It really didn't matter where she moved because crime was all over Atlanta, even in the suburbs,* I thought.

I wanted Mama to move because all her house would do for me was bring back old memories of Raymond kicking my ass. One time, Raymond and I were playing catch outside. I dropped the ball, and he beat my ass from the front yard all the way to my bedroom. No one was there to get him off of me either. Mama was at work, and Cynthia was away at a friend's house. I had never seen as much hate in a person's eyes as I saw in Raymond's. He didn't care that he was hurting me physically, verbally, emotionally, and mentally. He really had my mind fucked up. There were times that I had been too scared to go to sleep because, when he whipped on my ass, he would say, "I'm going to cut that damn hair when you fall asleep, you fucking faggot!"

I came back to reality and realized that Mama had changed her tone. She invited me to come with her and look at some houses in Duluth, which was a city in Gwinnett County. I told Mama that I loved her and that I would see her shortly. I laid across my bed and grabbed a notebook and wrote a poem called "It's Okay to be Gay."

It's okay to be gay,
And I can't help that I feel this way.
I can't help the fact that I look just like a girl.
Trying to be a man is just not in my world.
I know that God loves me and I know that He's real,
But another man's chest is what I want to feel.
I would love to slide my fingers up and down his back,
And I can't wait until he fucks me from the back.
I know that the first time is going to hurt like hell,
And Raymond said, "If you don't get right with God, you're going to HELL!"
Well, that's just a chance that I will have to take
Because, trying to be a real man, I can no longer fake.
I tried to be a man,
But it just wasn't in my plan.
I even tried to play ball,
But I want to dress in drag because I am so pretty and tall.
I want to be a lady and feel like a woman.
I want to have all of the sexy men.
If all of the men accept me for who I am,
Then Raymond needs to realize that I don't want to be a damn man.

I felt a sense of relief after I had written that down on paper. *This is what I will do,* I thought. *I will share my pain through song and poetry in drag.* I felt like I could take on the world. I felt like I could go a few rounds with Big Steve, but I was only kidding myself. He had kicked my ass back then, and he could probably still kick my ass. I went to the garage and hopped in one of Ronnie and Chris's cars. They had so many, and they said that I could drive them whenever I felt like it. Ronnie drove a black Lexus SC 430, and Chris drove a red Mercedes Benz C-Class. It was a wagon, and it was super cool. I got the keys off of the table to the Acura. It had leather seats, and the music was blasting. As I was backing out, I noticed what was playing— "I'm Coming Out" by Diana Ross— and laughed. I listened to the words, as she sang that she was 'coming out' and that she wanted 'the world to know'. *Is this a trick?* I wondered as I bobbed my head to the beat. *This song is about me,* I thought. I have to come out. *This is a sign from God. He's letting me know that it's time that I come out.* She even said that the time had come for her to 'break out of this shell'. That was it. I wanted to come out, but how?

7

Spending Time with Mama

I had enjoyed that song so much that I put it on repeat. I could picture myself in drag singing it at the Apollo. Or maybe I could go on *American Idol*. Nah, that would be a waste because Simon's smart-ass mouth would make me tell him off. As I got closer to Mama's house, I got more and more nervous. I had knots in my stomach. For some strange reason, I felt that Daddy was going to jump out of the bushes or something. I was so terrified of that man that I didn't know what to do. Raymond didn't tolerate that gay shit. Period. I turned the music down as I pulled into the driveway. Mama was at the screen door, looking at me.

She said, "Come on in. Let me fix you something to eat."

I hollered, "I already ate some fajitas earlier."

She locked the house up and got into the car.

"This is a fine automobile you have here."

"This is my teacher's car. He and his boyfriend have spoiled me rotten."

She had lost a few pounds. I noticed it first in her face. Then, I noticed it in the outfit that she had on. It used to fit her tight, but now it fell loosely on her. She strapped in her seatbelt and said, "Turn that up. I love this song."

I let the top back, and our hair blew in the wind as we listened to Diana Ross. She told me which direction to go. It really felt good to do something for Mama, considering that she had taken care of me all of my life. We both sat back and listened to the lyrics of the song. And I bet Mama was thinking that one way or another my ass was coming out.

When I finally exited the highway, we pulled up to a nice gated community. The houses were a mile apart from each other. Her neighbor would actually be a mile away. *Great*, I thought as I parked the car.

"Do you want me to stay in the car?"

"Why would I want you to stay in the car?" Mama asked as she closed the door. "I see that rose pink lipstick that you're wearing. Stop being silly, Trey."

I stepped out of the car, wearing a pair of tight skinny jeans and a tight Abercrombie shirt and a pair of canvas Vans.

"You will be my son until the day that you die. I wasn't ashamed of you when I knew it was you who was playing in my makeup, and I am not ashamed of you now. Trey, you are my only son, and I will accept any way you want to live your life. This is your life, and only God can judge you. I am here for you. I will always love and support you."

I hit the alarm and secured the car and grabbed Mama's hand as we made our way to the leasing office.

"You must be Mrs. Burns," the real estate agent said as she shook Mama's hand.

"And who might I have the pleasure to meet," she said as she turned and looked at me extending her hand for me to shake.

"I'm Trey, the lovely Mrs. Burns' son."

"Well, it's my pleasure to meet you both. My name is Sandy, and I will take you on a live tour. I understand, Mrs. Burns, that you already saw our virtual tour online, right?"

"Correct," Mama said as she looked at the huge chandelier in the ceiling of the model home.

I was amazed, too, because it seemed like it was so

far away. We walked outside and got into a mini golf cart and proceeded to go look at Mama's potential new house. I was so moved by Sandy's personality. She was so bubbly and very likable. She didn't look old, and forty is the new twenty, right? She was very hip, and she had a great sense of humor. As we rode up a hill, I noticed so many fashionable, stylish cars. I knew celebrities had to live out there. *Or, then again, it could just be a bunch of stupid, uppity-ass black people.* You know the ones who want you to think they *"have it"* when they are really in debt up to their fucking necks. We pulled up to a mansion that had to be ten times the size of Mama's house.

"Oh, my God," I said as I hopped off of the golf cart. "This house is to die for. Mama, I knew that you said you wanted the best, but— Dang!— I never saw a million dollar home in person."

"Well, this home was 11.5, but she's getting a steal. She's getting it for 5.8. You have the economy to thank for that," Sandy said with a big smile on her face. "So, shall we?"

She led the way, as she opened a big black gate. As we walked among the decorative trees that stood over us, Mama and I admired the garden area. Sandy opened the door, and I fell to my knees.

"I know this marble. This is some expensive marble," I said as I rubbed it like it was linoleum.

"It sure is, and it is worth about two hundred thousand dollars. It is African marble," Sandy said.

"Mother, we don't have to go any further."

Sandy looked at me and smirked and began to tell Mama about the amenities in the house. "This is a sophisticated Crestron smart home with computerized lighting, audio, and security. The gym is equipped with the latest gym equipment. And the sauna is adjacent to the elevators."

"We don't have to look no further," Mama interrupted. "I'll take it."

"Are you sure? Because I want to show you the flat grassy backyard with the in-ground pool. And there is also a gas grill out back that's great for grilling all year around."

"Yes, we're sure," I said as I fanned my face. "Just tell us where to sign, honey child."

8
Movin on Up

I was so happy for Mama. She was finally going to get her dream house. She was still young, and the lottery wasn't so bad after all. She'd been playing ever since I could remember, and it had finally paid off.

"Trey, are you going to move back home?" Mama asked as we headed to the car.

"Hell, yeah! I mean, yes, ma'am. I can't let you live in that seven bedroom house all alone."

"Well, we won't actually be alone. I also invited Cynthia and Jayson to come and live with us. We can be one big, happy family again. Without Daddy," she said as tears filled her pretty eyes.

"Mama, don't worry about Daddy. He'll realize what he has lost and come back home."

She looked at me and said, "I don't think he's ever coming back. He had so much hate and anger in his voice. It's almost like he's a different person."

"Mama, the devil is real, and he gets in people. And maybe it's good that he left. He might've killed us all. He's probably back in Jamaica where he belongs. I mean, I know that he's my daddy and all, but that man didn't show me no kind of love whatsoever. I can't even remember him ever telling me that he loved me."

"He loves you," Mama whispered. Mama just looked at him leaving us as a blessing.

"He almost beat my brains out, and for what? Because

I didn't want to catch a ball? I know it's not easy, but, Mama, we can live it up now. We can go shopping. We can get our feet and nails done. We can get our hair done. Just think about it, Mama. We're rich! You can get me some breast implants. Oops! Did I say that out loud?"

"You sure did," she said as she gave me a funny look.

I turned the radio up, and, once again, we both bobbed our heads to Diana's "I'm Coming Out." The more I listened to that song, the more I pictured myself looking like a full-figured woman.

"Let's go to Cynthia's," Mama screamed over the loud music. It had been a while since I had seen Cynthia.

When we arrived at her and Jayson's place, I was shocked because their house looked like a mini-mansion.

"I don't see why they have to come and live with us," I said as I got out of the car. *But, then again, maybe I could finally get Jayson*, I thought.

"She and Jayson are having financial problems, so it looks like I hit the lottery right on time," Mama said.

When Cynthia opened the door, I didn't even recognize her. She had definitely had some plastic surgery done. She looked how I wanted to look. Her breasts were a size 40 D, and she had the heart-shaped ass that I wanted. My blood was boiling inside.

"Hi, you guys," she said. She didn't even sound like herself. She sounded like Toni Braxton's sister Tamar of *Braxton Family Values* fame. I loved that show. All of the sisters were hot, even their mother Evelyn. But back to this heifer. How the hell did she just go and change up like that, knowing that this was the look that I had been going for all my life?

"So, where is Jayson?" I asked, trying to get my mind off of her sick body.

"He's out and about. He's hardly ever home. It's just

me and Princess here."

"Who's Princess?" I asked with an attitude as I looked her up and down, and noticed a pair of Christian Louboutin stilettos on her feet.

"She's my poodle, and she's so adorable. You will love her. She's such a doll. Come here, Princess," she said as she snapped her fingers.

Then, all of a sudden, a black blur came running towards us. I was thinking that maybe she had a little pug or a dog like Paris Hilton's or something, but she had a tall black standard poodle that had blue eyes. Not only was this dog groomed to perfection, it had on a Gucci sweater with an Amour Amour diamond dog collar around its neck. The collar was encrusted with real diamonds, and this one had, at least, ten two carats.

"No wonder y'all are having financial troubles, the damn dog is worth a million dollars."

"Actually, she's worth three million," she snapped back. "Jayson is never here, so all I do is shop until I drop and eat ice cream. This hair in my head is worth six thousand dollars."

"Too bad you wasn't blessed with my hair," I said as I slung my hair around.

"But I was born with these and this," she said as she grabbed her breasts and slapped her ass.

"Looks like a plastic surgery job gone wrong," I said as I looked at her seventy inch plasma television that was on the wall.

"You wish that I was still the tom boy that I was back in the day. Maybe, one day, you'll see how it feels to be a real woman. Maybe, one day, you'll get a man like Jayson to treat you the way a real woman is supposed to be treated."

I just stood there, looking at my nails, ignoring her.

She was definitely getting under my skin. Mama just sat there quietly while we went at it like two sisters, instead of a sister and a brother.

"So, why is your man always out in the streets? Are you not doing what you're supposed to do to keep him at home?"

"You let me worry about Jayson, and you worry about Daddy killing your punk ass when he finds you."

I really wanted to dig those green contacts out of her eyes and put them in mine.

"This is a lovely poodle," Mama said as she tried to change the subject.

"She's my baby," Cynthia said as she rubbed the top of Princess's head. She rolled her eyes at me and said, "Mother, I think I'll stay here after all because I see now that Trey and I will never get along. So, can you just be a sweetheart and give me a loan?"

"Since when do you talk like that?" I said as I walked towards her, getting in her face. "Cynthia, you're trying too hard. Boo boo, take it down a notch."

"Am I touching a nerve?" she asked as she bucked her eyes at me.

Mama got in between us and said, "How much money do you need, Cynthia?"

"Five million," Cynthia said, looking me directly in my eyes.

"Now, wait a minute," Mama said. "You two were like a hand to a glove growing up. Don't you remember?"

"Yes, I remember how I used to have to stop him, I mean, her from getting her ass kicked all the time," she smirked. Then, she said, "Mama, I will be by to pick up the loan. Get this piece of trash out of my house."

There was no way she was getting away with talking

to me like that. I was going to pay her back, and I knew exactly what I was going to do. I was going to find Jayson and fuck him in his ass.

9
Bad Blood

It's on, I thought as I got in the car and slammed the door.

"Trey, Cynthia didn't mean any of that."

"Mama, will you stop trying to be the peacemaker for once? It's reality, Mama. It is what it is. Daddy hates me, and now Cynthia does, too."

But I couldn't, for the life of me, figure out why. Why was she so upset with me? I wondered if Jayson had told her that I used to flirt with him at school. We had been so close coming up, and, now, it was like she had a vendetta against me or something. *But two can play that game. If she wants to have bad blood with me, I will make her life a living hell,* I thought as I sped out of her driveway. When I turned the radio on, Diana Ross's "I'm Coming Out" was still playing, and I carefully listened to the lyrics. I was going to do exactly what the song said. I was going to come out and let the world know.

Cynthia just didn't know that she had fucked up. How dare she talk to me like that? Once we had been two peas in a pod, but, now, we were more like oil and water, and she had created this mess. During the drive back to Mama's house, I thought about Cynthia.

When we finally arrived at her home, I walked Mama to the door and saw that the door was wide open. In complete disbelief, we walked into her house and saw that it had been ransacked. *This wasn't nobody but Daddy,* I thought as I looked around.

"Mama, you can't stay here tonight. You can come over where I'm living until you close on your house next week."

"I've been living here for almost twenty years, and no one has ever broken into my house."

"Mama, no one broke in. It was Daddy. Can't you see? I believe that he's out to get us."

She told me to hold up a minute while she went into the house. It was dark, and I was scared as hell. I got in the car and locked the doors. The thought of Daddy running around like a mad man had me on edge. Mama came back to the car with a letter that Daddy had left. She read the letter out loud as we headed to my teacher's place.

Carolyn,
You made our son like this.
You should have spanked him instead of giving him a kiss.
Now, he's running around trying to be a damn girl,
But I will find him, and I will end his world.
You know how I am, and I can't help it,
And I will have to kill you, too, and get your life over with.
I can't let Trey think that the way he wants to live is okay,
And I know that God will judge him one day.
I had a son, and that was all I asked God for.
Now, he wants to run off to California and be a whore.
I'm going to find him, and I hope that it's real soon
Because I am going to stick him in his ass with a broom.

"He made a threat! We can have him locked up!" I yelled.

"Trey, you know that your daddy don't give a damn

about the police or a warrant."

She was right because, when I used to tell him that I was going to call the police on him, he would dial 911 for me and, then, hand me the phone. I would always almost piss on myself.

"Well, what are we going to do?" Mama asked.

"We have to leave town. He's going to kill us both. He said it bluntly in that letter."

"Trey, don't worry about him. We'll be just fine."

"That's easy for you to say. You've lived your life. I mean, you know I didn't mean it like that. Mama, I am scared. I have dreams, and now all my dreams might go down the drain because of Daddy and his psychotic ways."

"Trey, if it will make you feel any better I will give you five million dollars, too, and you can go to California and pursue your dreams."

I have a better idea. Why don't you come with me?"

"I will be fine living here in Georgia. I am going to do some traveling with Cynthia. I think that will be good for her since she's having relationship problems."

When she mentioned her name, I forgot all about Daddy's stupid ass. I wanted to go to Beverly Hills and get work done from head to toe.

When we arrived at Ronnie's house, we found him and Chris cuddled up on the sofa, watching a movie. Chris paused the movie and introduced himself to Mama. Ronnie stood up and said, "You two look like twins."

"I hope it's not too much, but Mama will have to stay here for about a week."

"No problem," they both said as they made their way back to the sofa.

"She's pretty," I heard Ronnie say as we headed to my room.

"I remember him," Mama said as she sat on my bed. "He is a very nice fellow to take you in. I mean, us in." She grinned. "I knew when I first met your daddy that I shouldn't have married him. He was a loose cannon back then, and he's a ticking time bomb now."

"What do you mean, Mama?"

"Trey, your daddy is the type of person that will kill himself and a few others if things don't go his way."

"Well, is he my real daddy?"

"Of course, he's your real daddy."

"I just asked because he is so damn mean, and I don't look or act nothing like him. I don't see him in me anywhere."

"Trey, he's your father. I wouldn't lie to you. He's just Jamaican, and he means what he says. He has strong beliefs, and no one can change that. That's how he was raised. I fell in love with him because he was so charming. He would rub my belly when you were kicking inside. He adored the fact that he was having a son. He wasn't too fond of Cynthia, though. I don't know why he only wanted to have boys."

"Could it be because he got hurt in college and wanted to live his dream through his boys?"

"That's true, but I don't know him anymore. He's definitely not the Raymond that I married twenty years ago, not writing a letter like that."

Then, Mama, suddenly, looked in her bra and said that the lottery ticket was back at her house.

10
Shit Out of Luck

We both jumped up and hurried to the car. As we passed Ronnie and Chris, they had both fallen asleep on the sofa. I grabbed the first set of keys that I saw, and, to my surprise, they were to Chris's Mercedes Benz. Once I cranked up the car, "I'm Coming Out" began to play. *This must be the anthem that they live by,* I thought as I backed out the driveway.

I thought about the heated argument that Cynthia and I had had earlier. There was no way that she was getting away with verbally abusing me like that. *I am going to have a voluptuous body, and she is going to be so jealous,* I thought. *I can imagine her face when she sees me for the first time. I am going to be way more animated and dramatic than she is.* I had so many plans for Mama's lottery money. First, I was going to get some ass shots. I wanted an ass like Nicki Minaj's. Then, I wanted to get some breast implants. Finally, I was going to go to that dentist who was famous for whitening celebrities' teeth in Beverly Hills. There was nothing like a brilliant smile. The teeth were the first place I directed my eyes when talking to people. Then, I looked at their eyes.

I didn't quite know what I was going to do with my big-ass dick, but I knew that I would look foolish with big boobs, a big booty and a big-ass dick. I would look like a circus act.

Mama nervously patted her hands on her knees. She was so shook, and so was I. We were rich for only a few days, but it could all be over if Daddy had taken the lottery ticket.

Fifty million dollars was a lot of free money. Mama had been playing that damn Powerball since I was in elementary school. And she had always said that she would get herself a mansion if she ever hit the jackpot. I remember Daddy saying, "Carolyn, once you hit the lottery, we're going to live it up in Jamaica."

I would always say to myself, *And that will be the day that I run away.* I didn't want to live with him in America. What the hell would I look like, living with him out of the country? Daddy was a nightmare, and he had made my life a living hell. There were times that I would stay up all night until he went to work. I was afraid to go to sleep. He had threatened to cut my hair when I was asleep on numerous occasions. He needed to be in a psych ward. His rules were so strict. For example, if I didn't practice football by myself in the front yard, he wouldn't let me drink juice or eat cheese on my sandwich. He was the craziest man in the world. And I wanted to get as far away from him as I could. That was why I wanted to go live on the West Coast.

I silently prayed to God that the lottery ticket was safe at her house as I drove eighty miles per hour, trying to get there. Even though it was about a thirty minute drive, we got there in fifteen minutes because I had floored that Benz. As I turned on Mama's street, we saw red and blue lights flashing. Then, as I pulled up closer, we saw that her house was engulfed in flames. There were fire trucks and firefighters all over Mama's house.

"Oh, no!" Mama said as she cried uncontrollably. We got out the car and asked what had happened.

"Who are you?" a fire investigator asked us as we walked up.

"This is my house," Mama said. "What on earth has happened?"

"Apparently, someone fell asleep with food on the stove. And everything in the house has perished including an unidentified man."

I grabbed Mama as she fell to her knees.

"Unidentified man? It has to be Raymond. My husband. He's the only man who could have been in there, but we were separated. I mean, he left me."

Mama was a bit confused, and she was starting to twist her words. As Mama wept, I was kind of glad that Daddy was gone for good. He was probably in hell because he had definitely been one of Satan's helpers. I didn't have to see him or his long dreadlocks anymore. He looked like Screwface from the movie *Marked for Death*. I held Mama as she continued to cry like a baby.

"I'm sorry for your loss, ma'am," the fireman said as he walked away.

11
We Got to be Strong, Mama

Mama and I walked slowly back to the car. We looked on as the firemen put out the fire. She was clueless. She thought that Daddy had moved on. First, he left her. Then, he wrote a disturbing-ass letter. Then, he came home to cook. Then, allegedly, while he was cooking, he fell asleep and burned up the house and himself. It just didn't make any sense. Something was not adding up. Our dreams had gone down the drain, just like that, in the blink of an eye. Mama wasn't really worried about the lottery ticket. She had fire insurance on the house, so she would be getting an insurance check. She was crying and saying that she wanted to just tell Daddy that she loved him one more time. She really did love him because they had been together for so long.

"Mama, we got to be strong for each other. We will get through this together," I said as I pulled off. I turned the radio off, and we rode back to Ronnie's house in silence. It was the longest ride ever.

When we got back to Ronnie's place, it was a little after midnight. Ronnie and Chris had opened the door. They had been waiting up for us.

"What happened?" they asked as they made way for us to walk in. "It's all over the news that your house was on fire."

Chris handed Mama a hot cup of tea and helped her sit down on the sofa.

"It's true. Raymond is dead. He fell asleep with food

on the stove," she said as she began to cry again. Her eyes were swollen, and her whole face was red from crying so hard. She was crying like she had lost her best friend.

"But didn't he move out?" Ronnie said as he sat next to her. "I thought you told me that he left you."

"That's what I thought, too, but, apparently, he needed food. I don't want us to be a burden on you," Mama said as she sipped the hot tea.

"Trust me. You guys are not a burden," Chris interrupted.

"I should have an insurance check as soon as possible. I also had life insurance on Raymond, so that will be another healthy check. All I have to do is go identify the body and provide the insurance company with a death certificate. And that will be so hard for me to do."

"Don't be silly," they both said. "We would never ask you for any money for staying here."

"I will be here for you, Mama," I said.

"You can count us in, too," Chris said as he grabbed Mama's hand.

We all sat there and comforted Mama in her time of need.

"I have to plan the funeral. I have to do all sorts of things now."

"All of this is my fault," I said as I walked up and looked out the window.

"Trey, don't blame yourself. I won't let you stand here and put the fault on you. Everything happens for a reason. I will be alright once I get those checks rolling in. I'm just sorry that you and Raymond didn't make amends before he died. I really wanted him to make up with you. I didn't want him to leave this world without telling you that he did, in fact, love you. Raymond was a good man," she said as she grabbed my hand.

"It's okay, Mama. I'll be fine."

I was standing there, trying to remember some happy moments with Raymond, but I came up empty. There weren't any happy moments with him. Ever since I could remember, he was on my ass about playing football. I wanted to ease Mama's heart by, at least, agreeing that Raymond was a good man, but there was nothing good about him but the food he cooked. The curry chicken and mixed vegetables was one meal that we all looked forward to eating. We would all gather around the table, just the four of us. Mama would lead us off with a prayer. Then, as soon as she said, "Amen," Cynthia and I would pig out. I guess that was a good memory, but I know what Mama meant. She had really wanted to see Daddy and me get along, but that didn't happen because he wanted me to play ball and I wanted to wear heels.

"Come on, Mama. Let's go into my room and get some rest. We have a long day ahead of us tomorrow. We have to go to the morgue, and we have a lot of other business to take care of."

"Yes, sweetie. Trey is right. Go on back there and prop your feet up," Chris said. "You've been through a lot, and, remember, you guys can live here as long as you want."

"Thank you so much," Mama said. "You guys are the best."

I fixed the pillows, so Mama could prop her feet up, but she insisted on sitting in the recliner. I knew that she was hurting inside, but there was nothing else that I could do.

12
Chris' Other Side

The next morning, the whole house was filled with the aroma of a delicious breakfast. My room was downstairs, a couple of doors down from the modern kitchen. When I got out of the bed, I stretched, and I noticed that Mama was not in the recliner. I was glad she wasn't there to witness the hard-on that was poking out of my pajama pants. As I was going to the bathroom to piss, I accidentally bumped into Chris in the hallway and so did my dick.

"I can release that big thing for you," he said as he zoomed his eyes on my dick.

I put on a fake smile and went on ahead to the bathroom. While I was in the bathroom, I thought about what Chris had said to me. And from what I could tell, Ronnie was in love with him. Or he could have been with him just for his money. These days, it seemed people got into relationships for all the wrong reasons. I wondered if I should tell him about the sexual advances that Chris had made towards me. Ronnie would always tell me all of the reasons why he loved him. He said that they were both thrown out of the house when they came out of the closet. They both decided to go to college, despite their families casting them out. And college was where they eventually met, and they had been together ever since, but he did tell me that Chris's dick was very small. He stressed to me that he was the one doing all of the fucking in the ass. He said that he was definitely not with him for the sex. He was in love with him for the person that he was. He was very caring and kind. And on top of that, he was pretty wealthy.

I shook the excess piss off of my dick and washed my hands. I brushed my teeth and looked at how beautiful I was.

"Look out, California. Here I come," I said as I winked at myself in the mirror.

I made my way to the kitchen, and, to my surprise, Mama was in there cooking.

"You're finally awake," she said as she scrambled some eggs.

"I should have known that it was you in here cooking," I said as I took a seat at the table.
"These two are always eating out. If it's not Fogo de Chão, then it's Milton's Cuisine and Cocktails."

"You're right about that," Ronnie said, "but your mama can throw down. She could be our personal chef if she'd wanted to."

We all laughed and looked on as Mama continued to cook.

"It's ready," she chimed, inviting us to have a seat.

"I'm already sitting," I joked.

Mama had cooked a big country breakfast. She cooked bacon, turkey sausage, cream of wheat, cheese and eggs, waffles, and buttermilk biscuits made from scratch. She had also made a gallon of freshly squeezed orange juice.

Chris made his way in and sat right beside me. *He can't be serious,* I thought. Ronnie sat beside Mama, and he said, "Let's all join hands as we say our grace."

Chris's hand was cold as he quickly grabbed my hand. As Mama said grace, Chris rubbed the top of my hand in a circular motion. *He is dead-ass serious,* I thought. I grabbed his hand, hoping that he would know that I was a bit uncomfortable, but that didn't do any good. He stretched his leg and hooked it around mine.

"Amen," I said as I interrupted Mama's grace.

"You never let me finish grace," she joked.

"I am just ready to eat this bacon. It's calling my name," I said as I jerked my hand away from Chris's from under the table. I looked over at Ronnie and tried to make eye contact, but he was too busy eating. He didn't notice any of Chris's odd movements at the table. Our legs were still locked, and I couldn't believe what he was doing right under Ronnie's nose. Mama wasn't eating at all. She was so depressed, but she had to do something to keep herself busy, so she cooked and kept the house clean, even though Chris and Ronnie were already two neat freaks.

"So, what do you guys have planned for today?" I asked Ronnie.

"We're going to have a boys' night out," Chris said as he continued to swing our legs back and forth.

"That's right," Ronnie said. "I would invite you, but you have too much on your plate right now."

"You can say that again," I said as I tried to untangle my leg.

Chris looked at me and said, "I sure wish that you could join us."

He had been acting strange ever since he saw my dick when they played that prank on me. He would wink his eye at me as we passed by each other in the house. He would always ask me if I wanted to go to the spa with him. And, of course, I would always say no. He was a complete whore. He was always trying to throw himself on me. And he was nowhere near my type. He kind of looked like Danny Devito with blonde hair. I liked sexy, fine men like Omari Hardwick, Michael Ealy, Idris Elba, and Boris Kodjoe. I started to get a hard on just thinking of that sexy-ass Nelly.

While Mama cleaned the dishes, I headed to my room. I ran a hot bubble bath in the huge garden tub. It looked like it could fit four people. I added some honey bath oil to my steamy water. My skin was soft, and I wanted it to stay like that. I had so many lotions to put all over my body. I laid back and placed an eye mask over my eyes. I put on some soft music and enjoyed the hot water. Just as I was starting to relax, I heard the door open.

"Who's there?" I asked.

Before I could take off the eye mask, I felt someone get in the tub with me. I snatched off the eye mask, and there was Chris with his pale white body and tiny pink penis. He splashed me with water.

"What are you doing in here? Where is Ronnie and my mother?"

"I suggested that Ronnie take your mother out shopping to cheer her up."

"Why are you doing Ronnie like this? Why are you trying to come after me like this? Ronnie loves you," I said as I tried not to stare at his little dick.

"I have my reasons," he said as he reached over and grabbed my dick.

Even though we were in steaming water, his hands were still cold as ice. My dick stood up and got hard as he massaged it with his hands.

"To tell you the truth, I have been thinking about this dick ever since we played that prank on you."

"I can't cheat with you. It's just not right. Ronnie is doing us a huge favor by letting us stay here."

"*We're* doing you a huge favor," he said as he rubbed his finger around the tip of my dick. I was starting to feel horny, but, at the same time, I was thinking about Ronnie's feelings. He pushed me back against the tub and started sucking my dick. I tried to stop him, but he insisted.

"Don't fight this," he said as he spit on my dick. "This is the fun part." He gave me a wicked grin. "Can you fuck me in my ass?" He continued to slurp and slob on my dick.

"I don't think that's such a good idea," I said.

"Well, your dick is already in my mouth, so you may as well fuck me in my pretty pink ass."

I must admit he was sucking my dick good as hell.

"Oh, it's a good idea," he said. "I have the connections in Hollywood, remember? You want to be a woman, don't you?" He gently sucked on my balls.

"Well, yes. I mean, I don't know."

"That's not what you've been screaming since you moved in. I can help your dreams come true. And, before you chop this big, pretty dick off, I have just got to have some of it. Oh, my God! You have such a pretty dick, and it tastes so good. I want you to fuck me like you've never fucked another man before."

"But I haven't fucked another man before."

"Oh, so, I'll have the pleasure of being your first," he said as he stopped sucking my dick to bend over.

"Where is your condom?" I asked.

"We don't need one," he quickly said, looking back at me.

I never thought that this would happen to me in a million years. I didn't have anything against white boys, but I just didn't want to fuck this one, and, to make matters worse, he was my teacher's man.

13

Should I Open My Big Mouth?

I couldn't believe how easily my dick went into Chris's ass. He was bent all the way over at the end of the tub, and water was splashing all over the place. He was saying the same things that he said to Ronnie and that was, "Fuck me hard, daddy. Give me all of that big black dick."

I fucked him harder and faster because the only thing that I could think of was Ronnie and my mother coming in and catching us. This was just flat out wrong, and there was nothing that either one of us could do to justify what we were doing. If they had come in, we would have been caught red-handed. While I thought about the consequences of what would happen if we got caught, he kept looking back at me and slapping himself on the ass, saying, "Fuck me harder, daddy."

It was hard for me to concentrate on an orgasm because I was nervous as hell. I was in my teacher's house fucking his lover, so I closed my eyes and thought of Omari Hardwick. I thought about him when he played in an episode of *Dark Blue*. I licked my lips and rubbed Chris's back and fucked him even harder as I felt my sperm at the tip of my dick. He was screaming my name loudly.

After I finally came all in his ass, he tip-toed out of the tub, grabbed his things and left. I looked at my dick, and it was still hard, but, after I ran cold water on it, it went down. I was so disgusted by what had just happened. I let the water out of the tub, cleaned it with bleach and ran some more steaming hot water. As soon as I laid back in the hot water, Mama knocked on the door.

"I will be out in a minute," I screamed.

She walked in and said, "Boy, you don't have anything that I haven't seen before."

She came in and sat on the toilet. "What were you doing in here swimming? Why is there so much water on the floor."

"Oh, I was singing in here, and you know how wild I am." I said the first stupid thing that came to mind.

She looked around and said, "You even got water on the vanity, but, anyway, that Ronnie is so sweet. We went shopping, and he bought me a lot of nice things. He told me all about his upbringing. He told me how much he loves you and how he wants to see you succeed in life. He is such a nice person. He really has a heart of gold."

As I listened to her, I wondered if I should tell her about Chris and me. I knew that I could trust her, but, since she liked Ronnie so much, I didn't know if I should spill the beans just yet. I changed the subject and said, "Girl, show me what you got."

After I had cleaned up the water, I headed out to meet Mama in my room. She had several dresses and, also, had Gucci bags and Gucci heels to match them all. I put one of her after five dresses on. It was a spider web dress, and she just looked at me and smiled when I tried it on. This was designed by Scott Henshall.

"What do you know about that?" she said as she straightened the spaghetti strap on my shoulder.

"Nothing much," I said as I looked at myself in the mirror. "Now, all I need is a pair of these," I said, placing my hands on my flat chest.

"You really want to be a woman, don't you?"

"Of course, Mama. Look at how pretty I am. You and Daddy created one beautiful human being. Look at these pretty, long legs, and look at my face. I look like a younger version of you. And listen to my voice. It's not even deep like how a man's voice should be. I'm sorry to break the news to you, but you know I've been wanting to be a girl ever since I was in kindergarten. Do you remember when Mrs. Robinson had a conference with you? She asked me what I wanted to be when I grew up, and I told her a pretty woman. She told you that you'd better change my train of thought."

"Of course I remember that conference. How could I forget it? I had to hold my tongue because I was about to curse her out." Then, she walked over to me and said, "Trey, I will be here for you no matter what. Always remember that you can talk to me about anything, and I do mean anything."

She had said that like she knew something, but I didn't know if I should tell her about Chris and me. I wanted to, but it just wasn't the time. She tried on her dresses, and we both looked in the mirror.

I said, "We could go for sisters," as we bumped our hips together. Chris and Ronnie walked in and watched us as we styled and profiled Mama's new dresses.

"You two look like twins," Ronnie said.

"Y'all sure do," Chris had the nerve to say. I looked at him and cracked a fake smile. I couldn't believe that Ronnie didn't know what a slut he had for a man.

"We're going out," they said, "so don't wait up."

14
Morgue Blues

When it was time for Mama and I to go to the morgue to identify Daddy's body, Mama was very distraught, but she had put it on hold long enough. I didn't see the rush because he was like burnt toast anyway, according to the way the fire investigator explained the fire to us. Daddy didn't have a chance. He was burned to a crisp. And throughout this whole ordeal, I didn't even feel bad that Daddy was dead. I could finally be at peace, and I didn't have to worry about Daddy kicking my ass as an adult. I mean, really, how would that look if my old man ruled my life as a full grown woman? I had to admit that I was crazy at times, but I couldn't help it if I had the looks of a beautiful woman. My bone structure lit up whatever room I walked into. Now, all I had to do was get some size double D's and a fat ass to go with it.

Mama put her hair in a ponytail, and so did I. Before we got in the car, I asked, "Mama, what do you think of what I have on?"

I had on a long body dress with a pair of flats.

She said, "Trey, you're slowly but surely coming out, but are you going to go through this whole woman thing full throttle? I mean, have you actually sat down and thought this thing through? Have you thought of the mental part of this ordeal? This is a big change. I mean, I am here for you no matter what, but this will not be a piece of cake. You're actually talking about having a sex change operation. Have you thought about the procedure itself? You're about to change your penis into a vagina."

As I took in all that Mama was saying, I thought about what she was saying. And I hadn't quite thought about the operation. The cutting, the healing and the whole new thing. I would have to sit to use the restroom instead of standing up. I wondered if Mama was just saying all of that to make me change my mind. Being a woman had been my dream for the longest. *I was born a boy, but I will die a girl*, I thought as I parked the car at the hospital.

Mama sat there for a moment before she got out of the car. She looked at the hospital and said, "I haven't been down here since Uncle Charles had his open heart surgery."

We walked into the hospital and got unusual stares from everyone. I could see why they were staring at my pretty ass, but Mama had just lost her husband. I walked to the information desk, smacked my lips, and said, "We're here to identify a body."

"Sure. That will be in the basement," the lady said, not taking her eyes off of the dress that I had on.

When we got downstairs, we waited in a small chapel. It was so cold down there; it felt like we were in Alaska. Mama cried as we took a seat.

I held her hand and said, "Mama, it's going to be okay."

It was bad enough that Daddy had died, but, now, she was sitting here at the hospital with her son, and, to make matters worse, I had on a damn dress.

"Are you ready to do this?"

"I am more ready now than I will ever be. This is a part of my life that I will have to close and never look back at."

I couldn't have agreed with her more. I just wanted to forget about my mean-ass daddy.

"Right this way," a man said as he entered the room.

After we both got up, the man looked me up and down and cracked a smile. *He wouldn't crack a smile once he saw me in my new body,* I thought. The more attention I got, the more I wanted to change into a female over night. I wasn't even filling this dress up. Wait until I sprouted out like a flower.

"Wait a minute," a lady said as she stopped us in the hallway. "I'm Detective Anderson, and we've been trying to notify you, but we weren't able to contact you. There is something that we have to talk about."

"What is there to talk about?" I asked as I rolled my neck. "All we have to do is identify the king devil, and that's it."

"Who are you?" she asked as she looked at her clipboard.

"Detective Anderson, this is my son Trey."

She looked me up and down and said, "Let's all go back in the chapel and talk."

I was tired of people giving me the eye. I didn't lose my cool; I just twisted on down the hallway.

"There is a case of mistaken identity. I'm afraid that the dental records do not match a Mr. Raymond Seymour Burns."

"Lady, are you trying to say that that wasn't my dad who burned up in that fire?"

"That's correct," she said as she turned her attention to Mama.

"What do you mean?" Mama asked.

"This was not an accidental fire. This was set intentionally, and the person did not die because of the fire. He was already dead and placed there."

My heart was beating in my throat. Daddy was still

alive and wanted us to think that he was dead.

"Who was it then?" Mama asked.

"Since this is still an ongoing investigation, I am not at liberty to speak to you about this at length, but I will tell you that whoever did this is a maniac. Do you know of anyone who would want to set your house on fire?"

"Well, my husband is a very dangerous man, but I can't believe he would do this."

"Yeah. He don't want me to be a girl," I intervened.

"Oh, I see, and, because of that fact, he killed a man and set your house on fire?"

"He wants us to think that he is dead, so that he can come after me once I become a fabulous drag queen."

"Do you have any pictures of him, so I can give them to the police department? He will not be a suspect. He will just be a person of interest."

"I'm afraid that every picture that I had of Raymond burned up in our house, even our wedding picture. I can tell you how he looks. He's about 6'4", and he has dreadlocks. His eyes are black. I mean, there is no room for the whites in his eyes. He looks so cold and hard. You can see his soul through his eyes."

"Do you know where else he might be? Where is he from originally?"

"He's from Jamaica, and he also has other crazy family members."

"Trey, that's enough," Mama said. "Detective Anderson, I don't believe my husband is capable of murder. All he wanted was for his family to be close-knit. He just wanted all of us to do right."

"Why did you look at me when you say 'do right'? Mama, this is me, and I will not change for you or my crazy-ass daddy. Now, what I have to do is get the hell out of dodge.

He has threatened me over the years, and he let it be known that he would choke the life out of me. He don't care about anyone but himself. I have dreams, too, and my dream is not to catch a damn ball," I said as I hit the table. "I did what he wanted me to do. I played in the past for him, didn't I, Mama?"

I was crying, and I couldn't control myself.

"Why wouldn't he just leave me alone?" I screamed.

Detective Anderson looked like she was lost. She looked like she didn't know what to do. I wiped my tears and told Mama that I would wait for her in the car.

15
Cousin Kym

"So, what are we going to do now?" I asked as Mama got back in the car. "Daddy is not only on the loose like some maniac, he's killing people, too."

"We don't know that just yet," Mama said as she put on her seat belt.

"It doesn't take a rocket scientist to figure this out. Mama, read my lips. D-A-D-D-Y is crazy, and he will do anything to get to me!"

"Trey! Knock off the nonsense, and let me figure things out. Where could he be?" Mama said as she searched the streets for signs of him.

"Well, Ronnie and Chris said that we were welcomed at their place as long as we need to be."

"That's nice of them, but, Trey, I need my own space."

"Well, I still have about four thousand dollars left from the money that you gave me. That could help you get on your feet."

She was shocked, and I could tell by the look on her face that she thought that I had run through the money a long time ago.

"I sure would hate to ask Barbara if we could live with her."

"Excuse me? Not we. I am straight where I am. Mama, you and I both know that that lady doesn't like me. And I can't stand her. I remember her always pulling me aside at family gatherings, telling me that, if I didn't stop twisting, somebody was going to bust my ass wide open. I really despise that woman. She never had any kind words to say to me. She needs to worry about her thieving-ass daughter boosting clothes and writing those bad checks. At least, I am real about who and what I want to be. She thought her daughter was away at college when she was really somewhere with her legs in the air, making more babies. Cousin Kym ain't nothing but a baby maker. She needs to teach her kids their ABC's instead of showing them how to be professional thieves. She don't care what their tender, little ears hear. She lets all of her kids know how she tucked a dress and stole it out of Macy's. I wouldn't be surprised if she was teaching them how to follow in her footsteps. I don't like Barbara and Kym, and Uncle Charles wasn't any better. I couldn't stand his Luther Vandross-looking ass either when he was alive. He told me one thing and did another. Seriously, Mama he used to tell me, "Don't be a punk," and I would catch him with different men. He always claimed they were co-workers, and one thing I know is that a punk can spot another punk from a mile away."

"You're right about that," she said as she laughed while pointing at a man twisting and walking down the street.

We lived in Atlanta, the gay capital of the world. The studs really called themselves boys. There was no shame in their game. They even covered their breasts, making them look like they had flat chests. I didn't see the point. If they wanted to be men, all they had to do was get a sex change.

"I want you to take me by Barbara's house, so we can talk."

"Please don't tell me that you think you need to lean on that lady because, clearly, you don't."

"Trey, she's still my sister, and I am down, and I really need to talk to her right now."

"Maybe, you're right," I said as I headed west on the interstate.

When we arrived in Adamsville, it still looked the same. When you're on the West Side, you definitely knew it. There were bums all over Georgia, but I mean you really knew when you were on the West Side. It seemed as though there were more people out walking the streets. Could it be that the people who lived in DeKalb County had more cars than the folks on the West Side? That was what it seemed like to me.

When I pulled up at Barbara's house, shit was still the same. She had a three-foot fence around her house, and mutts were running loose around her yard. I hadn't been to her house in a while, but I couldn't forget how her house looked. She had the worst-looking house on the block. Her roof was peeling, and her screen door was missing the screen. Her yard didn't have any grass. It was only red dirt. And, when it rained, the kids would play in the rain and track dirt on the carpet.

"This house still looks the same," Mama said as she got out of the car. "Can you believe that I was actually raised in this house? This house has been in our family for years."

"I can believe that Aunt Barbara was raised in this house, but not you. You have way more class than she ever will."

"She's still my blood, and we're all we got."

I slammed the door and followed Mama to the front door.

As Mama prepared to knock on the door, I advised, "We may as well walk on in. Look at the damn screen door."

"Is that you, sis?" Barbara asked, fixing her wig as she came to the door.

She opened the door and glued her eyes to my dress.

"Have a seat," she said as she locked the broken screen door.

Why lock the damn screen door? All somebody has to do is stick their hand on the other side and open it up, I thought.

"I'll stand," I said as I looked at the filthy sofa.

I was not about to sit on that dirty-ass sofa and get my dress stained. There were lollipops stuck to it and dried up piss stains from Kym's babies.

"It's good to see you, Trey. Is that a dress that you're wearing?"

"It sure is. Do you like it?" I said as I rolled my eyes at her.

"Your cousin is in the back, and y'all haven't seen each other in a while. Why don't you go back there and catch up?"

I didn't want to walk anywhere in that house. The front room looked like a twister had been through it, so it wasn't hard to imagine what the rest of the house looked like.

"Go on, Trey, and speak to your cousin," Mama demanded.

I realized that she wanted to talk to Auntie Barbara in private, so I headed through the hoarder's house. As I walked down the hallway, the aroma of piss hit my nostrils. I got sick to my stomach, and I felt dizzy. When I got to her room, she was laying on the bed with her legs on the wall. She was on the phone.

"Let me call you back, fool. My cousin just walked in." She got up and said, "Boy, what the hell do you have on? Is that a dress?"

"No! It's a dress," I answered sarcastically.

"Y'all scat," she told her four kids. "Get out of here!"

Her oldest daughter looked at me and said, "Are you

a fag or something?"

"Never mind, Chiquita. She's very outspoken."

I looked around her room and saw that she had numerous bags from places such as Macy's, Bloomingdale's, Dillard's, Neiman Marcus, and Target. Her room was a wreck, too.

"Why are you wearing a dress?"

"Because this is the land of the free and the home of the brave."

I didn't really have anything against her. It was her mother that I didn't like, but she was starting to act like her.

"What happened with college?" I asked with an attitude.

"College isn't for everybody. Just like football isn't for everybody," she said as she walked over to one of her shopping bags.

"You have a point," I said as I leaned against the wall.

"You can sit down. I know my room is fucked up, but don't act like you're too good."

"I'm good up against this wall," I said as I looked at the bags.

"Well, as you know, I am a professional booster. It ain't no secret. I am good at what I do, and it's not illegal until my black ass gets caught, so, until then, I am getting to the money. This is America, and there is so much money to be made. My kids go to school wearing Gucci, and I'm not speaking of that fake shit either. I can put you down, and you can make some money, too. I will let you do the easy part, and that's taking the merchandise back and getting gift cards."

"No, thanks," I said as I looked at the ceiling as if I wasn't interested.

"Well, suit yourself," she said as she looked through

her bags. "Oh, yeah. I was sorry to hear about your daddy, too. It was all over the news, and I'm glad that you and Auntie wasn't in the house when it went up in a blaze. I know you didn't care two rusty nickels for him, but you have my deepest sympathy. If he was my daddy, I would have killed him in his sleep. I wouldn't have been able to put up with all the beatings like you did. You are one tough cookie."

She walked over to me and rubbed my hair.

"I don't care to talk about him, and I don't need your hustle either. I am going to get a job at a hair salon. It's owned by a woman named Mikkos, but she prefers to be called Peaches."

"I know Peaches. Everybody knows Peaches because, if you ever want a total makeover, she's the one to go to. She, also, does make up, and she's very creative when it comes to eye shadow. She can do styles that no one else can do. When people go to her, and they don't know what style they want, she always creates something cute, and they are always beyond satisfied. They don't call her the Hair Doctor for nothing. She does the best twenty-seven pieces."

"What's a twenty-seven piece?"

"Boy, if you're going to do hair, you better get hip to the styles that are out. No one wants to wear a casket sharp hairdo. And what I mean by casket sharp is, no one wants to walk around like they're getting ready for their own funeral. Take my mama. For example, she's so used to wearing those old fashioned wigs. She even wears them to bed. I don't even know what her real hair looks like. I like braids. All I have to do is get up and go. I don't have to worry about any weave itching my scalp, and I don't have to worry about any glue pulling my real hair out, so you better get with the program because there is so much competition in Atlanta. You will be in competition with Tammie. She owns Hair Trapper Studio.

She's a master stylist, and she also does kids and men's hair, too. She's very fluent in weaves, natural hair, and she does makeup as well. One time, she did my makeup, and my own mother didn't even recognize me. She hooked my face up. One of her friends, who is named Big Peaches, often comes in there and livens things up. She is so silly, and she's always telling jokes. I really think that she should go downtown to Uptown Comedy Corner and tell a few jokes with Shawty Shawty. You will also be in competition with Porsche. She's a doll who I happen to absolutely adore. She does hair on the East Side, and she looks like a celebrity if you ask me. She's very pretty, and she keeps her own hair laid. Some stylists will do everybody's hair while their own hair looks a mess, but not her. She looks like money, so she attracts more money. She specializes in weaves, natural hair and in different haircuts, coloring techniques, and she can use the hell out of a razor! She actually cuts hair with a razor. Can you believe that? She's, also, known for wearing custom-made bangles and bracelets. If you see her, you will know it's her because she has a killer smile and a banging body. And I can't forget about my girl Tiffany E! She owns TrendSetters Hair Studio on Candler Road in Decatur. She specializes in all types of hair, and she, also, does the latest popular hair styles. She does makeup, too. She has a cute little girl, and her name is Diamond. As a matter of fact, all of her kids are nice-looking. All of her girls are very pretty, and all of her boys are very handsome. And the ironic thing is that all of her kids' names begin with the letter D. Have you heard of Step?"

"No. Who's Step?"

"Her name is Stephanie, and she can lay some hair, too. She has a salon called Motivations. She's done my hair in the past. She did my hair in styles that only I could rock. No one else could rock them because she was just that good.

She could do a person's hair based off the shape of their head. Those were the good ol' days. I used to make a killing in her shop, selling her and the other stylists my clothes, purses, and shoes. You name it; I had it. It didn't matter what I had for sell. They would buy it because they knew that I had the real deal, especially Lyn. She's a stylist there, too, and she has been in the business for years. I bet she could do a sew-in with her eyes closed. There is also a stud that works in there, too, and her name is Meko. She's short, and she has dreads that she adds color to according to the gear that she is wearing. She is so fly and very sexy to me. She dresses like she has her own personal stylist. She and Michael Jordan should definitely team up because she has every shoe that he has come out with. I used to go get my hair done every week just to see her, even when I wasn't selling my merchandise. There would be times when my hair didn't even need to be touched up. And Step would look at me and say, 'Girl, you ain't foolin' nobody but yourself. We all know the real reason why you come in here three times out of a week.' If *swaggeriffic* was a word, Meko's picture would be right next to it in the dictionary. I would even go to the clubs to see her perform. I still see her out and about when she goes to the Blueflame and Phase One. I don't like girls or nothing, but, if I did, she would be one of the first ones that I would get with."

"Sounds to me like you're a little bi-curious."

"Nope. Not at all. Trust me. If I wanted to be with a bitch, I would be with one, so enough about me. What are your plans? I see your skinny ass in this dress. What's up with that?"

"Well, as you can see, I am going to be a girl."

"Trey, that's easier said than done. You just can't wake up one morning and decide that you want to be a girl."

"I am not judging you, so don't judge me. I am not

telling you how you should clean up this filthy-ass house. I'm not telling you how you should have checked your smart-ass daughter when she disrespected me. I'm not telling you that your mama needs to throw that tired-ass wig away. I'm not telling you that y'all need to go to Home Depot and buy a whole new door. I'm not telling you that you need to buy Huggies, instead of those cheap-ass diapers that your baby is running around here in."

"Okay! Cool! I get your point. I was just trying to let you know that it's not that easy."

"I know that, Kym. I have been hearing that my whole life, but now that I am grown, I can do what I want to do. Can't you see that all I want is to be happy, and, once I have this transition, I will be one happy camper."

16
It's My Body

As Kym's mouth ran like a car motor, I got upset because I had just stressed to her that this was what I wanted to do.

"It's my body," I said. "You don't have to go through what I go through."

So, I assumed that she wanted me to snap on her again about her lifestyle. How could she tell me anything when she was living in filth?

"Trey, I really think that you should sleep on this."

"I've been sleeping on this for thirteen years now. I've been wanting to be a girl ever since kindergarten. I just had a gut feeling, and I am not ashamed to follow my dreams. These are my dreams."

Kym was older than me, and she thought that she just knew everything, but she didn't know anything about the drag world.

"Did you sleep on being a thief and having four kids by four different men? Did you sleep on getting arrested over a dozen times for the same stupid shit? Did you sleep on flunking out of college in the first semester?"

"How could you say all of those hurtful things to me?"

"All the things that I said were the truth, and the truth hurts."

"Well, I only want the best for you."

"If you want the best for me, you'd best butt out of my business— period!"

"Wow! You really want to be a girl, huh? That's cool, Trey. When you turn into this glamour girl, don't forget to shop with me. I will have you wearing the dresses that Charlize Theron wears on the red carpet. I steal nothing but the best, and, yes, I am proud of it," she said as she held up a black and white Gucci silk plissé dress. "I went all the way to the Big Apple for this baby."

"You steal out of New York City, too?" I asked as I took a closer look at the dress.

"I sure do. And I do everything all by myself. I have seen too many people get jammed up going with a group to boost and steal clothes. And I haven't gotten arrested in over three years, so you can call me a professional booster."

"Well, I guess I could," I said as I went to go find Mama.

Mama and Barbara were talking about old times in that nasty-ass living room.

"Do you want me to come back and pick you up later?" I asked as I held my nose.

Auntie Barbara was cooking chitterlings, so the whole house smelled like shit.

"Yes, that's a good idea," Mama said. "We have a lot of catching up to do. As a matter of fact, you can pick me up in the morning."

"You're kidding me, right? Mama, I know you're not about to sleep in this house."

It didn't do any good for me to pinch my nose because those pig intestines was something serious. I felt like I was about to throw up. I walked over and hugged Mama and kissed her.

"I love you, Mama," I said as I walked to the door.

"Your mama knows where she comes from. You're the one who's acting all high and mighty," I heard Auntie

Barbara say as I closed the door.

"Fuck this nasty-ass house and your ass, too," I said as I got in the car.

I turned the radio up and listened to my favorite song. "I'm Coming Out" was just the song for me. I envisioned myself on a stage, singing this song to millions of people. I had on a sleek cashmere Gucci dress. My hair was hanging down with spiral curls on the end. My make-up was flawless, and my diamond accessories matched the custom-made diamond Gucci heels that I had on.

I decided to stop by Peaches' shop and let her know that I was old enough to work in her shop. When I pulled up, all eyes were on me as I popped the lock on the Acura. I walked in and noticed that she had moved her station all the way to the back, so I strutted my lanky ass down the red carpet like I was at the Emmys. I felt all kinds of harsh stares as I walked by, but that would be something that I would have to get used to.

"Hey, boo," I said as I went for a hug.

"How are you doing?" she said as she styled her client's hair.

"I am better than ever, and I am ready to work. You said, once I turned eighteen, that I could come work for you. I am going on nineteen now."

"What all do you know how to do?"

"I learned how to do a sew-in by watching video tutorials on YouTube."

"YouTube?" she asked as she stepped back and looked at me like I was crazy. "That's not good enough, so what you can do is be my shampoo assistant and watch me do hair. This is more hands-on than watching someone on the damn internet."

She was finishing up on her last client, and she was

about to close up her shop. I paid close attention to how she styled and curled her hair. When she was done, her client looked like she was a celebrity. She locked up her shop and looked at me and said, "You'd look a lot better if you would just take some growth hormone pills."

It was nice to have someone give me some advice that I could use, for once. I appreciated that she didn't judge me.

"So, what are growth hormone pills? I thought that I could just go to the doctor and get a bigger booty and some breasts added on."

"Child, please! You don't have the slightest idea. Where did you get your information? On YouTube? I see now that I am going to have to school your young ass. If you're going for the girly look, you have to look like a girl. I mean you're very pretty, which is a plus, but, if you want an ass like mine, you'll need to take some growth hormone pills."

She stood up and lifted up her apron, so I could see her derriere. *Nice*, I thought.

"Now, to be honest, I think that you should look on the internet and find out the best pills to take. I have a very personal question for you. Are you going to be a she-male or are you going to get your penis removed?"

"I am going to be a one hundred percent woman," I said as I snapped my fingers. "I am not going to think about the surgery because something about it might make me change my mind, but I will go on the internet and find out the best growth hormone pills to take."

"Good luck," she said as I left.

I couldn't bear to let Mama stay the night at that house. I could, at least, get her a room at the hotel up the street. When I got there, everyone was outside. I mean the whole neighborhood.

"What's going on?" I asked as I walked up to Auntie

Barbara.

"Your crazy-ass daddy! He came and killed your mama!" Kym screamed out the door.

"He what!" I yelled as I fell down to the ground.

"Kym, shut up! She's not dead," Auntie Barbara interrupted. "She's lost a lot of blood, though."

"What happened?"

"It all happened so fast. I was in the kitchen putting some hot sauce on my chitterlings and, the next thing I knew, she was saying, 'I'm sorry.' When I turned around, I saw your dad, and he said, 'You're already dead to me, so this won't hurt one bit. Your neck with my razor from ear to ear, I will spilt.' I dropped my plate with my coleslaw and chitterlings and ran to her, but it was too late. I wish that I could have helped my sister. She's my oldest sister, and she's been there for me all my life, and I couldn't even save her in my own damn house. He cut her neck from ear to ear, but she's going to make it because, according to the EMS, he didn't hit any major veins or arteries, and he didn't cut her deep enough. I saw him as he ran out of the door. He didn't even look like he used to look. He cut his dreads off of his head. It looked like he had just taken the scissors and cut his dreads off one by one. He was wearing a big overcoat. He looked like a bum. His jeans were dingy, and he had on a pair of brown Timberland boots."

"Well, where is my mama?"

"She's on the way to the hospital. Trey, I know that we're not the best of friends, but please be careful because he said that he's coming for your gay ass next."

17
Where do I Go from Here?

I got in the car and sped off as I left Auntie Barbara's. I was crying as I left. I couldn't believe that Mama had almost died right under her nose. She didn't really care for me because I wanted to be a girl, but she showed her sympathy and love for Mama, and I had to respect that. She didn't want to see me dead or hurt, even though she disagreed with my lifestyle. Instead of going to the hospital right away, I went home to see Ronnie and Chris. When I got there, Chris met me at the door. He said that Ronnie had gone frantic, hysterical, and crazy when he heard about Mama and had rushed off to the hospital to be by her side, but Chris was cooler than ice.

"Why didn't you go to the hospital with Ronnie?" I asked.

"I had a feeling that you would come here, so I wanted to be here to comfort you in your time of need. Ronnie is fine, and he loves your mother more than he loves his own. And I love you like you're my boy toy."

"You can't fucking be serious right now! My mother is lying in a hospital bed, probably on her death bed. And you want me to fuck your ass!"

"Why not? I have been thinking about you ever since you fucked me in the tub? Plus, I have the means for you to get away from your crazy-ass daddy. Trey, there are no limits to what we can do. What we do is our business. I have fifty thousand dollars in that briefcase. You could go to California and start your new life. It's such a shame that that big-ass dick of yours has to go to waste, but it's your decision. Now, can I please have just a little bit more before Ronnie gets home?"

"You're fucking serious, aren't you?" I said as I walked over to the briefcase. I opened it and saw that he was telling the truth. There was more than enough money in there to start a new life. "Come on. Let's get this over with quickly," I said as I closed the briefcase.

"We can do it right here," Chris said as he pulled his pants down.

I wasn't even in the mood to fuck. I had Mama and Daddy on my mind. He grabbed my dick and said, "Here, I will get it hard for you."

He put my dick in his mouth and sucked on it. I closed my eyes and envisioned that he was Tyson Beckford sucking on my dick. Immediately, my dick got as hard as a rock. Then, Chris released my dick from his mouth, turned his back to me, and bent over.

"Remember, this is just between the two of us."

"Don't remind me," I said as I slid my dick into his loose ass.

He moaned and said, "Ooh, yeah! Daddy, give me all of that sweet black dick."

As I pumped him harder and harder, I was glad that I was done fucking his pink ass. I came hard and sat down on the sofa. My dick was still standing up.

"It looks like big boy has more squirting to do," he said as he grabbed my dick, releasing some more sperm.

He went over to the briefcase and said, "I'll add another fifty thousand if you promise that you'll keep in touch with me once you move to California. I want you to be my boy toy."

I looked at him and said, "I don't get you two. If you're not in love with Ronnie, why won't you just leave him?"

"Oh, I am madly in love with him. I am just getting revenge."

"What did he do to you for you to do this to him?"

"For starters, he fucked your sister's husband Jayson."

"You guys were really serious? I thought that that was all a part of the practical joke that y'all played on me. So Jayson really is a fag? No wonder he didn't get mad at me when I flirted with him in school."

"Trey, I hate to be the bearer of bad news, but Ronnie has been fucking Jayson ever since he was in the tenth grade."

"You can't be serious," I said as I pulled my pants up. "The tenth grade?"

"So, what do you say? Are you going to take me up on my offer? I would love for you to be my boy toy."

"Sure," I said, not considering the fact that I was going to have a vagina and not a dick anymore.

He went to their bedroom and returned with the extra cash.

"You can have the Acura, too," he said as he walked towards me to kiss me.

I had never kissed a man before. *Hell! I'd never kissed a girl before,* I thought as I scratched the top of my head. *Maybe, he can be my sugar daddy.* I went to my room and packed a few things. I retrieved the money that Mama had given me. I sat on the edge of the bed and cried. Through my tears, I cursed God.

"Damn it, God! If you knew I wanted to be a girl, why didn't you just make me a girl from the start and make Cynthia a boy. This is not how I pictured my life. Mama is lying in the hospital because of me. She didn't deserve that treatment from the man who she thought loved her. I don't know what to do."

I wanted to go see Mama, but I had a feeling that Daddy would be watching the hospital. Plus, I didn't know how much longer I could keep a straight face around Ronnie. I had fucked his lover twice, and the guilt was sinking in, but, when I thought about the fact that he had fucked Jayson, the guilt subsided. I packed the dresses that Ronnie had bought for Mama.

"She won't be needing these anymore," I said as I put them in my suitcase.

As I walked to the door, I heard Chris say, "Don't forget our deal, boy toy."

I sat in the car because I didn't have a plan. I couldn't just up and go to California. I didn't even know anyone in the Sunshine State. Then, it dawned on me. *I will get a room downtown and learn how to do hair from Peaches. That's it! Then, after I become a master stylist, I can open up my own shop in California.*

I had more than enough money to get on my feet, but the problem was I was so damn young. I drove downtown and went into the Ellis Hotel and was quickly turned around by the night clerk.

"Sorry, kid. You have to be twenty-one years of age to rent a room."

"But I have money, lots of money."

"I'm sorry, but I can't risk it," he coldheartedly said.

My first thought was to call Chris and to ask him to get the room for me, but I didn't want him to be my unwanted guest every night. I dragged my feet back to the car. Then, I had a bright idea. I went to Lenox Mall and bought a push up bra and a long black shiny dress. I grabbed some makeup and applied it in the bathroom. As I was on my way to the car, a girl stopped me.

"Excuse me, but would you like me to help you with your face?"

"What the hell do you mean? Could you help me with my face?"

"Wait a minute. That didn't come out right. Let me introduce myself. My name is Flame… Flame Watts, and I am a mobile makeup artist. If Looks Could Kill is the name of my company."

"Oh, okay. I'm Trey, and, boo, I was about to curse your ass out."

"There's no need for all of that. I just hate to see makeup abuse," she said as she handed me her business card.

"You look nice," she said as she glanced down at my Giuseppe Zanotti Star Jeweled T-Strap heels on my feet. "Hold up! Wait a minute! You need to go back in the mall and get your feet done. You are messing up those gorgeous shoes. Where are you on your way to? Are you going to sing in a gay pageant or something? And is this a Gucci dress?" she asked as she felt the silk.

"Yes! Everything I have on is real. You sure are nosy," I said as I looked at her short manicured gel nails.

She didn't even stop to take a breather. She just went on asking me question after question. Then, I started to give her a questionnaire like she had just given me.

"Are those Versace shades that you have on? And where are you going all dressed up looking like Strawberry Shortcake?"

"Oh, I see what you're trying to do. You're trying to give me the third degree like I am giving you, huh?"

"Yep! You hit the nail dead on the head," I said as I looked down at my feet.

"Well, I was on my way to a club, just a few blocks

from here. Like I said, I am a mobile makeup artist, and I am going to makeup your kind of faces."

What do you mean by 'your kind'?"

"I don't have to have a PhD to see that you're a drag queen. I mean you'd look better if you had a booty pad and some breasts. I really think that you should enter the show. I think you would really fit in down there. Now, let's go back in this mall and get those toes done."

18
The Night Life

I thought, *This girl is crazy*, as I sat down and prepared to get my feet done. She suggested that I take off of my expensive outfit until we got to the club. She didn't bite her tongue for shit. Everything that came up came out, and I liked that about her. I didn't bite my tongue either, but I knew how to be humble.

She was short and a little on the plump side, but she was dressed to kill. She had on a hot pink Chanel cocktail dress with black ribbon trimmings with a pair of calfskin, two-tone Chanel pumps. I felt awkward sitting there with a towel across my legs. The Chinese women in there were speaking their language to each other, and I knew, for a fact, that I was the center of their conversation. They were giving me confused looks, but I kept my cool. I didn't get mad. I knew that they were talking about me, and I still left them a generous tip. I had known Flame for all of thirty minutes, and it seemed like I'd known her all my life. She told me that she had two kids and that they were the loves of her life. She was cool and definitely down-to-earth, so I happily followed her to Club Same Attraction.

"I don't have any identification," I said as I got out of the car.

"Oh, you're with me, and, when you're with me, you don't need any identification. How old are you anyway?"

"I am only nineteen, but I have big plans for my life."

"I know. You told me back at the nail shop," she said

as she straightened out her dress. "I still can't get over what you're doing with Chris."

"I was in a position where I had to do what I had to do, but I will figure out a way to end it."

"Your life is juicy and interesting," she said.

"She's cool," she said as we walked up to security at the door.

Flame addressed me as she, I thought as I looked around the big club. We went all the way to the back, to the dressing room, and, there, we found about one hundred men in drag. Some were tall, and some were short, but they all were very pretty. One of them even looked like Wendy Williams.

"I like this atmosphere already," I said as I looked on at the lovely ladies.

"Who will you be tonight?" one of them asked me.

"This is my first time here. I was invited by Flame Watts."

"Well, why don't you guess who I am tonight?"

I looked at her hard and, finally, said, "Mariah Carey!"

"Yippy! You're right. And these are my sisters Regina Belle, Patti LaBelle, Gladys Knight, Anita Baker, Betty Wright, Shirley Brown, Janet Jackson, Cher, Aretha Franklin, Peggy Scott-Adams, Denise LaSalle, Tina Turner, Chaka Khan, Whitney Houston, and the short one all the way in the back is Stephanie Mills. Whew! I am damn near out of breath naming all of y'all," she said as she turned around and looked at them.

I was so amazed by their beauty. They could go for those women for real.

Flame Watts had magical hands because she had done an outstanding job on their makeup.

I looked at Mariah and said, "Well, it seems to me that you've named all of the Queens of Soul, so I guess that leaves none other than the adorable Diana Ross."

Then, she turned her smile upside down and said, "Sweetie, we used to have a Diana Ross, but she was the victim of a hate crime. She was new to the Atlanta area, and she was at the wrong place at the wrong time. She was beat to death with a brick because she was transgender.
It's a shame. God created all of us equally, but it's unfortunate that we have people in this world that despise our kind. We all stick together in here. We are like a clan, not the Ku Klux Klan. We're all like family in here, and, if you ever need anything, you can come to any one of us."

They welcomed me with open arms and open hearts.

"You should, also, keep this with you," she said as she held up a leather keychain that contained a nine ounce can of mace pepper spray. "When you're out there in the streets walking with those high stilettos on, you have to think quick and spray a motherfucker. It has worked for all of us."

Then, she turned and walked to the other girls.

By the time Flame Watts was done with my face, I looked just like Diana Ross. Flame walked over to me and said, "I told you that you would fit right in down here."

"You were right. I love it down here. All of the girls are so sweet and nice to me. I just hate that I am so damn young."

"You should be glad that you're young because, as you get older, life will kick your ass, so don't rush life," she said as she dabbed a little more blush on my cheeks.

"Guess who?" I heard a familiar voice say.

I turned and looked, and it was my cousin Kym with a whole bunch of hot merchandise in both of her arms. She walked over to me and said, "You must be new. I haven't seen you in here before."

"It's me, Kym! Trey!" I said as I slung my hair back.

"Trey? My cousin Trey? Boy, stand up and let me look at you! You got titties and a butt that quick?" she asked as she felt my plastic breasts.

Stephanie Mills walked over and asked Kym if she had her yellow Chanel bag.

"Here you go," she said, not taking her eyes off of me. "Bitch, you look just like a woman. A pretty woman, I might add."

She got her money from Stephanie Mills.

"Turn around. Where did you get this dress from? I could have gotten it for you for the low-low." Kym looked at the tag in the back and said, "It's real, too."

"Of course, it's real, and it was a last minute thing."

"Why didn't you tell me that you did shows?"

"This is my first time. I was invited by Flame Watts. Do you know her?"

"Who don't know her? She's always all over town, doing makeup. She's a go getter, just like me. I'm so sorry about your mama. Your daddy is one sick, twisted son-of-a-bitch. I got a speeding ticket, trying to catch him," she said, showing it to me. "He was flying in a red Mercedes Benz. I never did like your daddy anyway. There was always something about him. One time, I spent the night over there with Cynthia. And he and your mama had got into an argument over you, and he slapped her so hard that her earrings flew off."

"That's not true. My daddy never hit Mama."

"Yes, he did, cousin. I swear on my right hand to God. Your mama didn't want you to know that you were the cause of all of her ass whippings. There were plenty of nights when she came to our house with black eyes. Cousin, look at me. I would not lie to you about something as serious as this." She had tears in her eyes.

"I believe you," I said as I dried her tears. "So, are you going to stay and watch me perform?"

"What kind of question is that? Of course, I am. We're blood. I wouldn't miss this for the world. Besides, do you remember that sexy-ass stud Meko that I told you about?

"How could I forget her? You bragged about how much you liked her?"

"She's the host for the show tonight. And I already checked her out. She has her dreads colored like the rainbow with a True Religion shirt, True Religion jeans and a pair of custom made rainbow Jordans. She is so damn sexy to me."

"Well, why don't you fuck her then?"

"I just might do that," she said as she reached in her bag and pulled out a small black Gucci clutch. "Here, cousin. You can have this one. It goes with your dress."

"Ladies, you have about ten minutes until show time," Meko said as she stuck her head into the dressing room.

"Hey, Meko," Kym said with the biggest smile ever.

"What's up?" she said as she smirked with those slanted eyes.

Then, Meko looked at me and said, "I will need your entry fee to enter the contest."

"I'll pay it for you, cousin," Kym said as she gave Meko the money and, embarrassingly, held her hand for far too long.

"Kym, I think you have a little sugar in your tank."

"You think so?" Kym said as she looked at Meko and licked her lips.

"Y'all are tripping hard," Meko said with a smile before she left.

"I thought about switching to the other side, but I don't think a girl will be with me with all my damn kids. Hell! I can't even find a man to be with me. And then there's my mama, always talking about how all gay people are going to hell."

"Well, first of all, don't put yourself down. You have to choose them. Don't let them choose you. And if you want to be with a girl, that's your business. You're on this earth to please you and only you. You can't worry about what people say. Take me, for example. I am standing here in a damn dress with six inch heels on. This is what makes me happy, so, I say, follow your heart."

"Thanks, cousin. That was a good pep talk."

"So, are you going to ask Meko out?"

"If I do, you'll be the first to know. Now, let me get out of here and go grab a seat. Everyone loves Drag Night. There's definitely going to be a full house tonight. I normally sit in the front row, so I can see Meko up close and personal. She has the cutest smile, and she always smells so good. She wears my favorite cologne— Issey Miyake."

"If you don't ask her out, I am going to ask her for you," I said as I looked at my gorgeous self in the mirror.

"No, cousin. Don't do that. I got this," she said as she left.

"Are you ready?" Flame said as she walked over to me. "You look nervous as hell."

She put one of her hands on both of my trembling hands.

"I am a little nervous, but all you girls have made me feel at home, so I will do what Mariah told me. She told me, right before I go out on stage, to say a quick prayer. She said it works for her every time."

All of the girls did an amazing job, and all of them got standing ovations. Right before it was time for me to go on stage, Meko told everyone to give it up for Big Peaches.

"Now, everybody in here knows that Big Peaches goes

hard every week when she performs her songs," Meko said before handing the microphone to Big Peaches. "Everybody, give it up for Big Peaches!"

The crowd went wild. Everybody was hyped up and ready to have a good time. She was suited up from her head to her feet. She wore a purple and white Adidas suit with a pair of custom made Adidas tennis shoes that had her name engraved with real purple diamonds. She had on a pair of Moss Lipow shades. The frame was alligator and ostrich leather. They were super fly. Tammie had also hooked her hair up with a slanted bob with a streak of purple in the front. She rocked the crowd as everyone rapped along with her as she shined and sweated on stage. Just as she was about to get off stage, a girl in the crowd booed her. She took out a stack of one hundred dollar bills and slapped the girl in the face with them.

Meko grabbed the microphone and said, "I bet your ass won't boo nobody else."

Big Peaches, then, looked at the girl and said, "The next time you hear grown folks rapping, shut the fuck up!"

Meko grinned as she told the crowd that I was a newcomer and that she wanted everybody to give me a warm welcome. She told them to make sure that they made me feel at home. She said, "Everybody, put your hands together for the astonishing Diana Ross!"

I said a quick prayer before I hit the stage. It was so crowded in there. I stood there for a moment to let the crowd take me all in. Then, I looked up at the bright lights just before I began to sing Diana's "I'm Coming Out".

I clapped my hands together with the microphone. And so did the crowd. They mimicked every move that I made. *This is so easy*, I thought as I walked to the edge of the stage. I heard Kym say, "That's my cousin, y'all," as she looked around at everyone near her.

Everything went perfect, and I don't know why, but, for some reason, I had thought that the crowd wouldn't like me. This was my dream, and it had finally come true. I had dreamed of this moment my whole life, and it was such a good feeling. As I sang my heart out, I looked in the crowd and I saw a familiar face looking at me. I dropped the microphone and ran off of stage because that man was Daddy.

19
Running Scared

I ran backstage so fast that my feet came out of one of my heels. I knew that was Daddy. I knew his eyes. I would never forget his eyes. I was so nervous. I felt like my world was about to end. All the girls ran after me and, when they caught up with me, asked what was going on with me.

"I had stage fright," I said as I looked at my surroundings.

I lied because I didn't want them to know that my daddy was as crazy as hell and that he would kill everybody in that motherfucker.

"But, sweetie, you were doing such an amazing job," Mariah said.

"I have to get out of here. I need some air."

As I ran out of the dressing room, I bumped into Flame Watts.

"What was that?" she asked as she moved out of my way.

"I will get up with you later. I have to get out of here. He will kill me," I said as I sped out of the back door.

I was relieved to know that security was in the back.

"Sir, can you please walk me to my car? I will give you a one hundred dollar tip."

"Hell, yeah! I will carry you to your car for a Franklin."

He picked me up and took me to my car. I laid my head on his shoulders and inhaled the cologne that he was wearing. He was tall and built, and his teeth glistened in the darkness.

"My name is Frank, and you can call me anytime," he said as he gave me his business card. "You seem frightened. What's going on?"

I had a feeling that he wanted to talk, and in the dark was the last place that I was trying to talk to anybody.

"I will be sure to call you as soon as I get to where I'm going."

"You make sure you call me tonight, and let me know that you've made it home safe."

He was looking so handsome in his security uniform. I admired men in uniforms.

I went back to the Ellis Hotel. I parked across the street and walked in holding my briefcase like it was a baby in my arms.

"Will anyone else be joining you, ma'am?" the night clerk said.

I looked around to make sure that he was talking to me.

"No," I said as I looked back to make sure no one was following me. "I would like to rent the presidential suite for about a month." I opened my briefcase.

"The presidential suite runs about two grand a night," he said with one eyebrow raised.

"That's fine. I'll take it," I said as I looked around the quiet lobby.

"Are you famous?" he asked as he looked at the computer.

"Not yet," I said with a smile.

I couldn't believe that he didn't recognize me from earlier.

"Just fill this out. Will that be cash or charge?" he said as he handed me a pen.

"Cash, always cash," I said as I handed him sixty thousand dollars.

"Are you sure you want to pay that much for a room?" he said as he loosened his neck tie. "I have a house that you can buy for ten thousand dollars."

"I don't have a choice. I need somewhere to stay tonight."

I didn't want to put other people in harm's way, so I looked at him and said, "Yes, I am sure, and I will need around the clock security. Do not. I repeat. Do not let anyone come to my room."

"Yes, ma'am," he said as I gave him the guest check-in sheet. "I knew that you were famous." He punched my name into the computer. "It says here that you're Diana Ross."

I guess it was true that white people really thought all black people looked alike. I was relieved to see that security cameras were all over the hotel.

When I got to the fifteenth floor, I threw my briefcase on the floor and closed the thick curtains. I put a chair behind the door. I looked at the card that Frank had given me, and I decided to give him a call. I looked around the suite and smiled. It was a tiny piece of heaven. I was speechless as I looked around at the exquisite room. When I called Frank, it was almost daybreak. I called Bob at the front desk and told him to let Frank up. When Frank got to the door, he had a bouquet of red roses. I opened the door and put them in a vase that had artificial flowers in them. He definitely put a smile on my face.

"So, what's a pretty girl like you doing down here all alone?" he said as he took off of his jacket.

I could see his muscles as they rippled through his T-shirt.

"I have dreams, and I am trying to follow them. I am

almost twenty, and I have had a hard life."

"The girls told me that you ran off the stage. While you were performing, I peeked in on you, and you were doing a wonderful job."

"Oh, about that, um…" I stuttered as I got up and put the chair back behind the door.

"You don't have to put that behind the door. I am here to protect you," he said as he put the chair back at the table. "Now, what are you so afraid of?"

"How do I know that I can trust you?"

"If I wanted to do something to you, I would have done it by now, don't you think?" he said as he grabbed my face and looked deep into my eyes. "Now, please tell me what's going on in that pretty little head of yours."

I looked away from him and looked at the picture on the wall. I broke down and told him my whole life story. He came closer to me on the bed and held my hand as I continued to pour my heart out to him. He smelled so good, and I was feeling so vulnerable. I was so depressed. I was thinking about Mama; I was thinking about the confrontation that Cynthia and I had had. I wished that I could get Daddy off of my mind, but he had my head fucked up.

"I understand," Frank said, "but, if your daddy is such a maniac, he should be behind bars."

"My daddy don't care nothing about no damn jail. He will do anything to get to me."

"I can't believe that he sliced his own wife's throat," Frank said, shaking his head.

"I want to go visit Mama so bad, but I am scared that Daddy will be there waiting on me. I know for a fact that he was in the crowd. I know my daddy, and I will never forget his demonic eyes."

I really enjoyed Frank's company. He was single, and he was originally from Philly. He was twenty-eight years old, and he owned his own security company. He didn't have any kids, and he'd never been married. He was a stand up guy, and he said that he liked *my kind,* too. He understood that I wanted to have a sex change operation, and he told me that he would be there for me every step of the way. He said that he really admired my honesty and my beauty. He accepted me for who I was, and he said that he had fallen in love with my bedroom eyes.

20
Suite Times

Frank and I had become a couple. He didn't have a problem with me wearing a booty pad and fake breasts. He admired my body with or without the attachments. I wasn't ready for sex with him just yet because I wasn't sure if I wanted to get fucked in my ass. He was the perfect gentlemen, though, and I really wished that I could take him around Cynthia and show him and his biceps off.

In the short time we'd been together, we had ordered so much food from Ruth's Chris Steakhouse that I had gotten thick in all the wrong places. My shoulders had started to broaden, and I was no longer skinny like a string bean.

I still had plenty of money left, and Frank had employees working for him. I really liked him, and the more time we spent together, the more we fell for each other. He never really told me why he'd chosen me over a real woman. I guess some men just had their preferences. *Maybe, he never wanted kids,* I thought. We lived in the suite like it was our home. It was just like our home. Bob had given us a monthly fee of one thousand dollars per month to continue living in the luxury suite. He really thought that I was the real Diana Ross. Bob didn't allow anyone to come to our suite, not even housekeeping.

I called the hospital once I got settled in my suite and checked on Mama. I learned that she was still in a coma. She had lost a lot of blood when Raymond sliced her neck. I really wanted to go and see her; I wanted to hold her hand, but the nurse told me that Auntie Barbara was by her side. I wanted to talk to Kym and let her know that I was alright, but I didn't know if I could trust her.

I didn't even see her when I ran out of the club that night, but I bet that she was still hustling and making her some easy cash.

Frank told me that I should write in a diary because I had a lot on my mind. He really understood the inner me. He didn't judge me, nor did he criticize me, and I loved that about him. When we took bubble baths together, he caressed my back. He was so good to me. He even distinguished my fantasy from reality. He said that he thought that I was just infatuated with heels and the whole dressing up thing, but I assured him that I wanted to be a woman. Then, I asked him if he would be with me if I was a man or a woman. He said that he would be with me if I was either/or. It didn't matter to him. He had fallen in love with my heart. He had fallen in love with me. I had fallen in love with him because he was so understanding. I mean this man didn't mind my fart if I let one go in the room. He was the right man for me. I decided to do what he said, so I bought a diary, but I didn't write in it right away.

Frank and I decided to go to AMC Fork & Screen Buckhead and watch a movie. When we got there, we got so many stares. The sky looked so blue, considering that I had been in the suite for almost five months. We walked hand in hand, and I didn't care about any of the stares or dirty looks that people gave us. All that mattered to us was each other. He kept a smile on my face, and I kept one on his face.

We sat down in the movie theater, and I was amused that they were serving food in there. He ordered some wings, and I nibbled on a few fries. He ordered a stiff drink, and I sipped some of his strong Hennessy. After a short while, I felt kind of tipsy, but the feeling was a good feeling. We went to see Tyler Perry's *For Colored Girls*, and, to my surprise, Omari Hardwick was in it, playing a gay man.

"Oh, my God! That is my favorite actor! I am so like in love with him!" I said as I rubbed Frank's chest. He didn't get jealous; he just chuckled and continued to watch the movie. I rubbed on his dick, and it was hard as hell. The alcohol was really doing a number on my head.

"Let's finish this at home," he said as he kissed me and grabbed my hand as we left the theater.

"How about I suck on it until we get home?" I said as I staggered to the car.

"You can have your way with me," he said as he unlocked his two door black Porsche.

His dick is huge, I thought as I tried to deep throat it with my tiny mouth. My head was spinning, and I thought that I had better stop watching so many damn flicks. I realized that I couldn't do everything that I saw on TV. *Those bitches on flicks are pros, and this damn alcohol has got me into trouble*, I thought as I sucked on his dick like I knew what I was doing. There was no way that I could take his big-ass dick in my ass. *I have a hard time shitting when I'm constipated.* I laughed a little at that thought. It was funny as hell to me.

When we got to the suite sooner than I expected, I thought, *How in the hell am I going to take all this dick in my ass?*

21
My Diary

When I woke up the next morning, Frank was not there. I felt my ass, and it wasn't sore. I looked on his side of the bed and found a letter. He told me that he had to run a couple of errands and that he would be home later. I held my head as I looked around the room.

"Did we have a fucking party or something?"

I saw an empty bottle of Hennessy in the kitchen.

"What the hell happened last night?" I asked as I stumbled to the bathroom.

I didn't remember shit. I called Bob and asked him to bring me a bottle of aspirins. I took four aspirins and decided to write in my diary after all.

February 1, 2012

Dear Diary,

I really don't know what I feel or what I want. I do know that this is where I am supposed to tell nothing but the truth. I am feeling Frank, but I am starting to feel that I don't want to be a woman anymore. I am so confused. One minute, I want to be a girl, and then, the next minute, I want to be left alone. So, what on earth do you call that? Am I one twisted individual or what? Maybe, Daddy is right. Maybe, I should be a man. Maybe, I should put some bass in my voice. Maybe, I should cut my hair.

When Daddy and I used to practice catch, I never caught

the ball, and Daddy would go to work on my behind. Sometimes, Mama was there to save me, and, sometimes, she wasn't. Either way, I can look back and remember Daddy saying, "You're going to let Cynthia outdo you? She has more balls than you, and she's a girl!"

I would just ignore him and go in my room and blast the radio. Mama would come into my room and baby me. And then Raymond would say that I was going to be sweet.

"You have to stop letting him have his way."

Then, Mama would say, "He's my baby, and he will grow out of that."

"He's going to be a fag," my dad would say with hate in his voice.

Daddy would come out of the room sometimes after he and Mama would have sex. He would say, "Trey, you're supposed to be into pussies not dicks."

I hated when he talked to me like that, but there was nothing that I could do but take the abuse. There was another time when Mama wasn't at home and Daddy told me to come and ride with him. I was scared, and I thought that he was going to kill me. He took me to a hotel room. When we got there, a lady was already in the bed. I stood at the door, shaking like a leaf.

Daddy looked at me and said, "Boy, you're going to fuck her. And I am going to watch. I believe, if you feel what pussy feels like on your dick, you'd want to be a man."

"You can't be serious," I said as I looked at the whore in the bed.

My dad didn't know that I had already had sex with Trish just a few days earlier, and I don't know why I didn't tell him since the whole school knew. I guess I was just too afraid to defy him there in that hotel room.

"I am dead-ass serious," he said as he threw me on the bed with her.

"Where's my money?" the woman asked as she looked at Daddy.

"It's right here," he said as he held up three crisp fifty dollar bills.

"Come on, sweet cheeks. I have other tricks lined up," she said as she scratched a white pimple by her mouth.

"Daddy, please don't make me do this," I pleaded.

"Son, this is only right. God made men to be with women, not men. Now, put that condom on and fuck her."

I was crying, and he didn't care. He told me to lie down on my back. I did what I was told, but I couldn't get hard. Then, the woman grabbed my dick and put it in her mouth.

She said, "There. That's hard enough."

She put the condom on me and rode my dick.

"How does that feel, son?" Daddy asked as he sat next to me on the bed.

I had tears coming out of my eyes, but he didn't care. All he said was, "Son, I am trying to make you a man. I am trying to save your soul from going to hell."

I was crying so much that I didn't even notice that Frank had come in.

"I see that you decided to take my advice and keep a diary," he said as he handed me some Kleenex.

"Thanks," I said as I dried my tears. "It hurts so much."

He hugged him.

"Thanks so much for being with me. I couldn't ask for a better companion," I said.

He brushed my hair back with his hand and said, "Just think of me as your guardian angel."

"What happened last night?" I asked as I walked over and grabbed the Hennessy bottle.

"You don't remember?"

"No. I don't remember anything. The last thing I remember was seeing Omari Hardwick on a big screen."

"Do you remember us leaving the movies?"

"No."

"You had a few too many drinks, and you started fidgeting with me. We didn't finish watching the movie. Once we got here, you started talking about your daddy, and you made me go and buy this bottle of Hennessy. You was telling me that you wanted me to kill your daddy before he kills you. You cried about your mama, and you said that you were going to pay Cynthia a visit. You were talking crazy last night. I even tried to stop you from drinking the whole bottle, but you were belligerent, so I agreed with everything that you said because you were actually trying to drive last night."

"Okay. That's enough. Please don't ever let me drink again. I was such an embarrassment, wasn't I?"

"It's all good," he said as he looked out the window at the city lights of Downtown Atlanta. "You were definitely feeling yourself last night."

"Well… did we? Did you…"

"No, nothing like that happened. We didn't have sex."

"You, on the other hand, went to sleep with my dick in your mouth."

22
Clubbing

It had been almost a year since I had been out to a club. Frank had talked me into getting out more, but, when Frank went away on business, I had no one to hang out with, so I had to find something to do.

Frank had always asked, "How long can you run from your daddy? You can't live your whole life in a damn presidential suite."

Mama wasn't doing any better, and I couldn't bear to see her like that. I prayed for her recovery. Just the thought of her lying there asleep, not knowing what day of the week it was cut me to the core. I blamed myself everyday and prayed that Mama would wake up from her coma. Even though I didn't physically do it to her, I still blamed myself because Daddy blamed her for the way that I was.

I put on a strapless Oscar de la Renta evening dress and headed to a club. I didn't know which club I was going to. I wanted to go see the girls, but I was sure that Daddy would know that I was there. I didn't want to make shit that easy for him, so I decided to go to a swingers' club.

When I arrived, I quickly grabbed my mask and put it on my face. I went to the bathroom and found Kym in there, selling her bags.

"Damn! She be everywhere," I said as I eased out of the bathroom.

I didn't want her to see me because I didn't know who I could trust. So far, Frank and Bob were the only ones I could trust.

I dropped the mask as I ran to get in my car. The night was still young, and I wasn't ready to go home. I wanted to have some fun, so I went to a bowling alley. While I was at the bar, a man walked up and asked if he could buy me a drink.

"Sure," I said as I quickly eyed the people who were bowling.

This is boring as hell, I thought as I looked around and saw kids running everywhere. I took the shot of Hennessy to the head and left. Finally, I decided to go to a club that was on the Eastside.

After I walked into the club, I went to the bathroom and looked at myself in the mirror. I had to make sure that all of my pieces were in place. I had to make sure my breasts were standing up in place and my booty pad wasn't crooked.

"Girl, do you see all of these niggas in here tonight? I am going home with somebody's son," I heard one girl say in a bathroom stall.

"Hell, yeah! I am right with you," the other girl said as she stood by me, looking at herself in the mirror. She smiled big as she looked at her grill for any noticeable food.

"Hurry up, Lisa! It's some wannabes in here," she said as she looked me up and down.

Lisa came out of the bathroom and washed her hands. She looked at me and said, "Y'all come to straight clubs, too? Damn! Y'all are trying to get all of the men. Hey! You with the booty pad on! I am talking to you." She tapped me on my shoulder.

"I am just here to have a good time. I don't want any trouble," I said as I moved her hand off of my shoulder.

She reeked of alcohol and onions as she said, "Y'all have all of the gay spots downtown, so go down there," she said as she staggered out of the bathroom.

That was a close one. I thought that I was gonna have to use my mace on her fat ass.

She really hurt my feelings, and I knew I shouldn't have been hurt so easily, considering how harsh Daddy had talked to me when I was younger, but I sat on the couch in the bathroom and cried. When I heard some voices and footsteps approaching, I tried to hide my tears, but I couldn't.

"What's wrong?" one of the women asked me as she walked in.

"I am a wannabe," I said as I continued to cry. I looked at her, and I immediately knew who she was. She was Porsha, the celebrity stylist from Decatur.

"You are very pretty," I said as I looked at her beautiful face.

She was light skinned, and she had a thin waist and a bad-ass shape to go with it. She looked like a life-size Barbie. She had on a black Versace dress with the heels to match. She had on expensive costume jewelry. Her teeth were perfect, and her makeup was flawless.

"What do you mean you're a wannabe?"

"I want to be a pretty woman just like you. I was born a boy, even though God knew that I would want to be a woman."

"Well, don't blame God," Porsha said as she lined her lips with a M·A·C lip liner. "You're still young, and you have your whole life ahead of you."

Then, she turned and walked out.

23
Miami Beach

Frank was still out of town on business, so I decided to check on Mama. When I called, the nurse told me that Ronnie was with her. She told me that Auntie Barbara had stopped visiting. I knew that Chris wanted to hear from me, so I was going to call him when I straightened things out. I looked around the suite and said, "I have to get out of here before I go crazy."

I went to the airport and hopped on the next plane to Florida. While I was on the plane, I thought about what Porsha had said. She said that I had my whole life ahead of me. I listened to all of her constructive criticism. She was definitely a woman of power, and she was very head strong.

I went to Ocean Drive and rented a room at the Betsy Hotel. I went to the patio and looked at all of the beach goers. Everyone looked like they were having such a good time. I took off my dress because I'd be damned if I'd come to Florida to get picked at. I put on a tank top with a pair of Polo swimming trunks and a pair of Polo flip flops. I looked down at my toes and realized that they were still polished.

"Oh, well," I said as I headed for the beach.

As I walked on the beach, I knew all eyes were on me, but I didn't feel a devious vibe. After walking through the sand, I went to the Pelican Café. Everyone seemed so friendly, and I figured out why. It was gay pride weekend, and I didn't even know it.

"Guess who," someone said as he covered my eyes

from behind.

His hands were cold, and I knew it wasn't nobody but Chris.

"I'm not mad at you," he said as he took a shot of tequila. "We had an agreement, and I know you're probably broke by now, so it's not a problem. I have a condo down on the beach, and I have plenty of cash. You were supposed to be my boy toy."

He rubbed his hands through his head as if he was frustrated.

"I was going to call you once I got myself straight."

"You look pretty straight to me," he said as he ordered another shot.

"Seems like you're too drunk to remember that I have been going through a lot. My mama is in a coma, and my daddy is trying to kill me, remember?"

"Ronnie is at the hospital with your mother."

"I know."

"How do you know?"

"Because I call and check on her every day."

"Ronnie told me that your mama came out of her coma and said this:

I gave birth to a boy not a girl
If your father finds you, that will be the end of your world.
How could something like this happen to my child?
All of those years that I've been in denial.
Trey, you're my son, and I love you so much,
But seeing you as a man, I'll never be able to touch.
So, Trey, if you've changed your sex, please change yourself back
Before I collapse and have a heart attack.
I saw all of the signs, but I never knew it would come to this,
But, you being a young man, I will surely miss.
So, son, if you hear me, please help my heart.

I've done my best to raise you, now please do your part.
This is how you want to live your life, but your father doesn't understand.
All he ever wanted you to be was a productive, athletic, young man.
Trey, you know that I love you no matter what,
But I don't want your life to be cut.
Everyone in the world will not accept your lifestyle,
And it doesn't matter that it was your dream as a child.
So, son, keep praying to GOD and make that change,
And I promise that GOD will hear you, and He will rearrange.
If you're doing it for the money, then that's okay
Because I want to have grandkids by you someday.
I really want us all to be a loving, caring family again.
Son, please look to GOD. He will always be there for you and be your friend.

I was in tears after hearing what Mama had said about me.

"So, she's out of the coma," I said as I jumped up for joy.

"Well, no. Not exactly. She slipped right back into the coma after she said that. I told Ronnie that you were in California. Why are you here in Florida? This is too close to Georgia. Your crazy-ass daddy is liable to be on the beach some-damn-where."

"Chris, I don't need this right now. I'm going to my room."

"I'm coming, too," he said as he followed behind me. "You checked into the most expensive hotel on Ocean Drive."

We walked into the room.

"I have an idea. Let's go to the Palace," he said as he flopped on the bed.

"What's the Palace?"

"It's a place where *our kind* can be free."

When he said *our kind,* I knew that he meant drag queens.

"Just get dressed and meet me back at the Pelican Café in thirty minutes," he said as he left.

I took a hot shower and wrapped my hair in a bun. I put on a stunning Barbie black and white pageant gown. It was skin tight, and I remembered how Mariah had told me to carefully tuck my dick. My dick was so big that I had to put on two penis tuckers. I looked at myself and knew that I looked gorgeous. I slid on a pair of black Maggie Christian Louboutins.

My eyes were smoke gray with a touch of metallic silver. I had watched Peaches do makeup and hair so much that I eventually got it down to a science. Some of those girls would come in the salon tore up from the floor up, but Peaches didn't call herself "the Hair Doctor" for nothing. She really did perform surgery on her clients' heads.

I walked to the Pelican Café as the sun was just about to set. I sat there, waiting for Chris. I looked around at my surroundings, and he was right— *my kind* was all over the place. They were even serving drinks from behind the bar. *This is where I need to move,* I thought. *Fuck California!* There were some people who had their alcohol all in the streets. It was so live, and I was enjoying every minute of it. Some people were drunk, and some people were just having a good time. Then, out of nowhere came this girl walking through the crowd saying, "I got Gucci bags, Versace bags, Louis Vuitton bags, Christian Louboutin bags, Michael Kors, Fendi bags, and they're all for the low low!"

"Hey, cousin," Kym said as she sat at the table where I was sitting.

"Damn, Kym! Your ass is in Miami selling shit, too."

"Hell, yeah! This is Gay Pride Weekend, and it's plenty of money down here. Look at all this drunk-ass money walking around. And didn't I tell you to shop with me? I could have gotten you that same dress. I steal drag queen pageant dresses, too. You still look pretty, though. So, did you have the operation yet?"

There she goes about to start asking me a million questions, I thought.

"It's been a while since I saw you. Why did you run off of the stage that night? Everyone really enjoyed your singing," she asked.

"I saw my daddy in the crowd."

"No shit?" she said with her eyes wide open as she put her micros in a ponytail. "It's a good thing that you did run because your daddy is like the Terminator. I'm headed to the Palace to sell the rest of these bags. You should come down there. The drag queens down there look like authentic Barbie dolls."

"That's where I am supposed to hang out at tonight with a friend."

"Cool. Then, I will get up with you when you fall through. And make sure you come. I have something important to tell you. I would tell you now, but I don't want to spoil your weekend."

I watched as she and her expensive bags disappeared into the crowd. I thought about what she had said, but she was right— I didn't want her to spoil my weekend. I was getting a bit irritated and impatient waiting on Chris. *Where could he be?* I thought as I twisted my way down the strip to the Palace.

24
All Drags Aren't Fags

As I walked down Ocean Drive, I observed how beautiful it looked. I thought about Mama, and I really wished that I had been there when she woke up, but I was happy to be in a crowd. In a weird way, it was comforting to be surrounded by so many people. When I got to the Palace, the line was so long, and *my kind* was everywhere. I looked around, and they had on some of the highest, biggest, and craziest wigs that I had ever seen. I'd only seen those wigs on RuPaul, and that was only on the internet. It was a thrill to see them up close and personal. The ladies smelled so good, and I blended right in with them. After standing in the line for some time, I was finally able to get in the club. I sat at the first chair that I saw because my feet were killing me. My Christian Louboutin shoes were very pretty, but they weren't made for walking. I saw Kym standing by the bathroom, hustling her hot-ass merchandise.

I was starting to think about what she had told me about all of the competition in Atlanta. After listening to her, I wasn't even sure if I wanted to do hair any more. Maybe I could design shoes or something. There were not too many black people that had their names on shoes. I could name my shoes Traynesha. *Nah, that's too long,* I thought. I have to think of something that's simple, short, and catchy. I could just name them Trey. That's my name, and I'm black, and they would be hot. The only thing that I would hate was if my cousin Kym got a hold of them and sold them on the streets for the low low. I quickly erased that fantasy out of my mind and went to the bathroom.

"Hey, cousin! I was just telling her about you," Kym said as I walked into the bathroom.

"Is that right? And what were you telling her about me?" I asked as I looked the girl up and down.

"I was telling her that you were my cousin and that you wanted a sex change operation. And she told me that she chickened out."

"And why was that?" I asked as I looked at her.

"I will leave you two alone and be sure you come and find me, cousin," Kym said before she wandered off.

"Hi! I'm Reece, but I go by Lady R. I changed my mind because I always worry about what people say about me. I don't know how not to listen to gossip when it concerns me. I took the growth hormone pills as you can see. These are my real breasts. See. Have a feel," she said as she grabbed my hand. "When I went to get a consultation for the sex change, I thought about my mother telling me that she wanted grandkids one day. And, of course, I am her only child, so what am I left to do?"

I took my hand off of her soft breasts and said, "So, in reality, do you want to be a girl or not? Do you like men or women? What are your dreams? I mean everyone in the world has dreams. I have a lot of dreams, and one of them is to become a famous drag queen. I also want to be a master stylist, and I want to be a fashion designer, maybe even design shoes."

She looked at me and said, "All of my dreams have been shattered. I wanted to be a girl at first, but it was too much for my mom. All I do now are these shows. They're not even that much fun anymore, so I do it for the money. I like to dress up like Anita Baker."

And she was very pretty, too. I guess that there were just some men that could go for women and that there were just some women who could go for men. She said that she had just lived her life as a girl and that she liked men. She said that she'd even gotten beat up a few times because the men liked the upper part of her body, but, when they felt down low, they would get angry.

She said, "Not all men are like that, though. There were some who accepted me."

And I could see why. She was very attractive.

After we exchanged phone numbers, I went to find Kym. I went to the front of the club because I knew, since Meko was hosting that night, she'd be right on the front row. And, boy, was I right. She was right there in the front row, staring at Meko. She had saved a seat for me, so I sat down and poured myself a glass of champagne.

"Look, cousin. There's Meko," she said as if she was a kid in a candy store.

"I see her," I said.

Meko was wearing a black Louis Vuitton jacket with the letters *LV* cut into her mohawk dreads. I couldn't really see the outfit because it was dark, but, from what I saw, she was fresh from head to toe.

I entered the pageant. For my talent, I decided to read a poem. I didn't feel like singing that night. The first contestant to go up was Lady R. She grabbed the microphone, and she slung her hair in and out of her face. I thought she was having a seizure at first, but Kym told me that that was all a part of her performance. She sang Anita Baker's "You Bring Me Joy". And, my God, she sounded and moved just like Anita.

"Bravo!" I said as I stood up clapping my hands, looking around as she finished. I didn't see any sign of Daddy or Chris.

The next person to go up looked like Tina Turner. Her wig was wild, like she had rolled it with firecrackers. She started clapping her hands and stomping her feet. Then, she sang the words to Tina Turner's "I Don't Wanna Fight". And all I could do was think about Daddy kicking my ass.

I looked at how well she worked that stage, like she was the real Tina. Her legs were big and pretty just like Tina's, and her face lit up the stage with the L'Oreal Rebel Red lipstick that she was wearing. I couldn't even tell that these women were men. They were all so beautiful.

"Guess who," Chris said as he covered my eyes from behind.

I know those cold hands anywhere, I thought, but I wasn't prepared to see what I saw as I turned and looked at him. He was in drag, and he looked exactly like Cher. He was just a tad bit shorter. Other than that, his makeup was flawless, and he looked gorgeous.

"You look fabulous," I said as I stood up to hug him. "I didn't know you dressed in drag."

"Only when I come to Miami," he said as he looked at my cousin Kym.

He had on a fuchsia fringe Latin dress with the hips cut out. He looked like a real woman.

"So, do you like?" he said as he sat down.

"Of course, I like," I said as I looked over to introduce him to my cousin Kym, but she was too busy looking at Meko on the stage.

"So, are you going to go up and do a song?" I asked him.

"Of course, I am. I'm not looking this stunning for nothing. Look at these Maggie Christian Louboutins that I have on," he said as he lifted up his leg for me to see.

"Those are hot," I said as I lifted up my feet, so he

could see that we were wearing the same shoes.

He had on a white pair and I had on a black pair. He looked at me and said, "How else did you think I was going to dress, coming to this fabulous club? And it's no secret that I am the woman in our relationship."

"Has Ronnie ever dressed in drag?"

"Child, please! I can't even get Ronnie to put on a pair of Speedos."

We laughed and enjoyed the show until it was time for us to go up. I was talking and laughing with him so much that I didn't notice that Kym was gone.

Chris went on before me and sang Cher's "Believe". I clapped my hands and noticed that he had a nice voice and a set of lungs on him. He wasn't moving off beat either; he was rocking with every beat of the song. He was hitting high notes, and, when he finished, he got a standing ovation. I stood up and clapped my hands, looking around. I didn't know where Daddy was, but I had a strange feeling that someone was watching me. I didn't see any sign of Daddy, and it was my time to go up.

I grabbed the microphone and said, "I want to switch things up tonight. I want to say a poem if that's alright with you guys."

"Go right ahead!" the crowd yelled.

"A friend suggested that I write down all of my thoughts and fears in a diary. I took his advice, and this is a poem that I came up with. And it's called 'I'm a Drag, not a Fag'."

I'm a Drag, Not a Fag.
All of my life can't fit in a bag
This is my life, so just let me be.
I can be a woman if I want to be.

God loves me, and He loves you, too.
Let Him judge me and not you.
I am so proud of the skin that I'm in.
I'm on this earth to do one thing and that is to win.
If Mama could accept me, then, Daddy, you should, too,
Because all I ever wanted was a relationship with you.
You saw my traits as a girl growing up,
And Mama would always cover them up.
I can't help that I'm as pretty as can be.
I even look better than some real women. Just look at me.
I will run from you all my life if I have to,
And, Dad, I just want to say that I love you.

25
Chris

Chris and I mingled and socialized with the other drags in the club. Some of them were transgender, and some of them were just like me, dressing as a woman. I had heard so many horror stories from so many of them. Some of them told me the worst, and some told me the good. I preferred to hear the good, but they all told it like it was, neither one of them sugar- coated anything.

I had gotten tired of listening to some of their nightmares. I would just have to see for myself if I wanted to be transgender or not. Chris and I really enjoyed ourselves. Kym had suddenly disappeared, and there was no telling what she had gotten into. Chris was a cool dude, but I wanted to be the bitch, but he wanted me to fuck him like he was the bitch. Technically, he was in his relationship with Ronnie, but I guess that was the meaning of being a boy toy. I guess that there were just certain things that I had to put up with, and fucking Chris's pale ass was one of them.

Chris and I gathered our big purses and headed to his condo on the beach. It was bad enough that he reached under the table to play with my dick. We walked down Ocean Drive, and everyone was still partying like they didn't have a care in the world. Dressing up in drag in Miami was the least of my worries. I was worried that Daddy would catch me and kill me. Chris assured me that I had nothing to worry about. That was easy for him to say. He didn't have a maniac chasing after him, trying to kill him. We entered on the west wing of the Bentley Bay Condos. We got on the elevator, and he pressed the thirtieth floor. I thought, *The higher, the better.* When we arrived inside of Chris's condo, it was everything that I thought it would be. I walked in and looked at the patio, and I immediately noticed the panoramic view of downtown Miami. The floors were imported and made of stone covered with limestone marble throughout. His condo was ocean front, and I felt like I was in heaven. *I could get used to this*, I thought.

Even though Chris had promised me so many things, I was still taking Ronnie's feelings into consideration. Chris had a fat-ass bank account, but, by *all* means, he was not my type.

"Come on over here," he said as he sat on the dark gray Santa Barbara sectional sofa.

"Come and sit right here next to papa," he said as he snatched his wig off.

I walked over to him, slipping my shoes off one by one. I sat on the sofa, and he didn't waste no time jumping on me.

"Can we get out of these dresses first?" I said as I eased him off of me.

"Sure," he said as he got up and quickly took his off. "You know that I am so in love with you."

"You are like triple my age. How the hell can you be in love with my young ass?"

"Well, put it like this. I am in love with your big, pretty-ass dick," he said as he groped at my dick.

He was so forward, and he knew exactly what he wanted. He didn't seem to even care for Ronnie any more. He made me think that it was all about me. I bent him over, and we did the usual. I fucked him like a bunny rabbit and hopped off of him. We were both gasping for air, looking up at the ceiling. He finally got up and fixed us a cold glass of sweet iced tea.

"Here. This should cool you off," he said as he handed me an expensive white tea cup.

"Does everything you own have to be name brand?" I said as I took a sip of my tea.

"Hell, yeah! I work harder than Donna Summer for my money, and you will know that once you start designing those fancy shoes you told me about."

"I don't know what I want to do with my life," I said as I detached the fake breasts from my chest. "I don't want to do hair anymore because there's so much competition out there. I don't know if I got what it takes to design a damn shoe. I don't even know if I want to go on with this transgender shit. I am so confused, and I wish that Mama was here with me."

"Trey, we can do whatever we want to. All we have to do is stick to our guns and do them. Now, about this transgender thing, I think that you should go get a consultation and see if this is what you really want to do."

All of a sudden there was a loud bang at the door.

"Hurry! Hide in here," Chris said as he led me to his huge walk-in closet.

"Why are you hiding me? Who is that?"

"You're really asking me questions right now? Are you serious? It could be your crazy- ass daddy."

As I looked around in the closet I was surrounded by all different types of heels, purses and wigs. *He wants to be a girl, too,* I thought as I looked at the Jimmy Choo shoes organized according to heel length. I have watched enough crime television to know that a knock like that on the door could not be nice. All I could think about was an episode of *The First 48*. Those episodes were real, and they were very scary. They never had happy endings, and no one ever survived. I kept on thinking that someone would kill me and that I would rot in this expensive-ass closet. *Well, at least, I look like a girl,* I thought as I shifted my plastic breasts. I got on my knees and prayed. And, if I didn't learn anything from Mama, I learned the power of prayer. Just as I finished, Chris opened up the closet door and said, "Come on out, Scary Jerry."

26
Who's There?

"Who was that at the door?" I asked as I slowly eased out of the closet.

"Oh! That was just this beauty right here," he said as he pointed at a baby palm tree. "I forgot that these were to be delivered this week. This baby is incredibly rare, and I have been waiting on this for almost a year."

"Well, what the hell is it?" I asked as I walked closer to it. "It looks like you could just go pick one of these out of the ground in downtown Miami."

"This is very rare," he said as he held it like a newborn baby. Then, he looked at me and said, "This is a cycad or you may know it as a Sago Palm."

"I don't know it as anything," I said as I picked one up.

"Did you have to order so many?" I said as I looked around the living room.

The floor was covered with them. It looked like we were somewhere in the wild.

"These will fit perfectly on my spacious patio."

He grabbed as many as he could, and so did I.

"They need to be out by the light post," I said as I joined him on the patio.

"Don't be silly," he said as he gave me a slight tap on my ass. "These are very unique plants, and I will treat them like they're my kids. Oh, this is for you," he said as he slouched down on the sofa.

He handed me a small white envelope.

"Where did you get this from?" I asked as I sat down next to him.

"The delivery guy gave it to me."

"The delivery guy! Well, did you ask him where he got it from?"

"Of course not. I was too busy looking at his muscles. You should have seen his abs through his shirt."

He was in a daydream, and I was in shock with the anonymous letter in my hand. *Who could this be from?* I thought as I sniffed the letter. No one knew that I was in Miami, not even Frank.

"What are you smelling it for?" Chris asked. "If you're trying to see if you smell anthrax, you're wasting your senses because it's odorless."

"Duh. I know that. I'm not stupid. I smell a familiar fragrance on here, though," I said as I walked over for him to take a sniff.

"It smells good," he said. "Now, hurry up and open it."

I carefully looked at the envelope and held it up to the light. Mama used to always do her mail like that, and then she would say it "didn't look like a check".

"Hmmm… no return address," I said as I opened the letter.

As soon as I opened the letter, the fragrance hit both of our noses. It was so strong. The handwriting was in cursive, and I noticed that some of the words were smeared by the loud smelling fragrance, but I still made out what it said. It said:

Another Woman's Man
Feeling like a helpless bird lying on its stomach with one broken

wing,
I was thinking, Why did you have to fuck my man last spring?
It was wrong, and you couldn't have thought that it was right.
He used to come home and cuddle with me real tight late at night.
Being with my man is the wrong fucking answer.
You need to go somewhere else and be another man's private dancer.
You got the right plan, but the wrong man is what they say,
But, when it came to my man, you should have just turned the other way,
But I trust my man, and I know that you made the first move,
But I will kill you before you make your next move.
I hate it when little tramps like you try to take what I got.
I have a nice man, a big house, and you will never take my spot.
I've seen you do things out of the blue,
And guess what!? You don't know me, but I know you.
There are so many bitches like you that are so damn sleazy,
And you don't even put up a fight; you're just too damn easy.
You are trying to get away with things and be slick,
And you get on my damn nerves. You make me sick!
I see you walking and twisting in those expensive shoes,
But just remember one thing, bitch. I will not lose.

"Who did you piss off?" Chris asked as he snatched the paper out of my hand.

"I have to get out of here! This paper clearly states that someone is following me."

"Who could it be?" Chris said as he followed me to the door. "Well, whose man did you fuck? And where are you going? You are my boy toy."

He had turned pink in the face.

"Look! I will call you, Chris. Don't you see that I am in danger? Not only do I have to worry about Daddy, now I have to worry about a crazy psycho bitch, too. I don't know where I am going. Just don't follow me please. It's too dangerous."

"Please call me," Chris said as he planted a big, wet kiss on my lips.

When I went to my hotel room to get my money, I found that the room had been ransacked. The first place I looked was under the bed, and all of my money was gone. I was scared as hell, but I had to get out of Miami, and I needed my money.

I needed Mama more than ever. She was always my problem solver, but she was lying up in a hospital bed all because of me. I had no choice but to go to Cynthia. *She couldn't hate me that bad,* I thought as I signaled for a cabbie.

I nervously looked around as I got into the cab.

"No bags, ma'am?" the African taxi driver asked.

"No bags. Now could you please hurry to Miami International Airport?" I said as I strapped on my seatbelt.

When I got to the airport all eyes were on me, and my eyes were on them, too, because I was looking to see any familiar faces, including Daddy's face. It didn't matter that I was filling up the fabulous dress that I had on. I knew that they'd seen a fucking drag queen before. The nerve of some people. They didn't even have the audacity to look away or talk about me under their breath. I ignored all the dirty stares and headed to buy myself a ticket back to Atlanta. I looked at every single person's face that boarded the plane. No sign of Daddy. I felt a sigh of relief once I sat in the window seat. I felt secure, and, at ease, there was no sign of my crazy-ass daddy. I listened to the flight attendant tell all passengers to put on our seatbelts. I really didn't see a point. Once we went down, that would be the end. I never heard of a seatbelt saving anyone in a plane crash, but those were the rules, so I put on my seatbelt anyway and put on a pair of ear phones to watch the in-flight movie. I sat back comfortably, and I was glad that the movie of choice was *The Bodyguard*. I loved Whitney Houston in that movie. She was such a diva. I remember when Mama used to walk in on me. I was always in her heels, and I was always singing Whitney's "Saving all my Love for You."

Whitney Houston had a voice like no other, and I was very saddened by her death, but Mama used to always say, "When somebody dies, it's because God knows best. And, sometimes, God picks flowers for his garden sooner than others."

So, Whitney was now with God in Heaven, singing for God and his angels. I really loved her music. She was so real, and her music really touched my soul. She was such a powerful singer. The world had really lost a special soul, but, where she was at now, all souls were free.

"Rest in Paradise, Whitney," I said as I sat back and dozed off.

27
Rear Entry

When I arrived back in Atlanta, I was so glad to see my city. This was the city of dreams, but my dreams wouldn't come true as long as Daddy was breathing.

And I was smelling like two day old clothes. I was looking like a star, but that didn't stop my underarms from stinking. I was in desperate need of a shower. And I knew just the place to go to take a hot shower. I needed a bath. And my feet were throbbing in my heels. I was so thankful that I had a few thousand in my fake breasts. It was funny how I had learned so many things from Mama. Mama used to put up her "Lord, have mercy money" in her bra. I didn't learn shit from Daddy. I was glad because Daddy was mean as a rattlesnake. I didn't want to be mean to anyone unless I had to be.

When I arrived at my suite in Downtown Atlanta, Bob was waiting for me and was still as friendly as ever. I walked past him as he checked in some new guests. When I got to my suite, I heard some music playing. The door was cracked, so I slowly opened it and noticed that red rose petals were all over the floor, leading to the bathroom. The room smelled of vanilla and cream, and candles were lit everywhere. The room looked different as I closed the door.

"Who's there?" I heard a woman's voice ask.

I know Frank don't have a bitch in our room, I thought as I walked to the voice that I heard.

"Who the fuck are you?" I said as I looked at the

woman in the tub.

"I am the guest who just checked into this room," she said as she grabbed her robe.

"This is my room," I said as I looked around and didn't see any of my belongings.

"I am waiting on my husband. We just got married," she said as she stepped out of the tub.

I ran to the door and noticed that I was in the wrong damn room.

"I am so sorry," I said as I headed for the door. "I've had a long week, and I got the numbers twisted."

"I'm a Christian, so I will forgive you this time," she said as she locked the door behind me.

I went to my room, and I looked at the door number to make sure I was at my suite.

"Finally, home sweet home," I said as I opened up the door.

As soon as I turned the knob, I felt a grip on the other end of the door. It was Frank. I had really missed seeing his masculine body.

"Baby, I missed you," he said as he closed the door behind me. "You just left me without a warning."

I thought, *You left me*.

"You look so pretty," he said as he helped me get out of those painful heels that I was wearing.

"I had to get away. I took a much needed vacation."

"Well, I could have gone along with you. I have to talk to you about something," he said as he kissed me.

"Does what you have to tell me have anything to do with this letter that I got from your bitch?"

I threw the letter at him and watched as a strange look came across his face as he picked it up.

"First of all, I have been nothing but truthful with

you," he said as he stretched out the paper. "There is no other bitch. I don't even like to refer to women as bitches, but, since you said it, I am just repeating after you. This is not from anyone that I know. Baby, look into my eyes and believe me when I tell you that I am in love with you and only you."

For some reason, I believed him, and he didn't question me either.

"I have a surprise for you. I want you to marry me, and I will pay for your sex change operation."

He knelt down on one knee and handed me a four carat diamond ring.

"Will you marry me?" he asked as he looked into my eyes.

My eyes watered up, not because I was sad, but because I was overjoyed.

"Yes, I will marry you," I said as I let out a huge laugh.

He really did love me, and I believed him when he said that he knew nothing about that letter, but it still puzzled me as to who it could be. We kissed, and he laid me on the bed.

"I seriously have to take a shower," I said as I tried to get up.

"I will join you," he said as he led the way to the shower.

He turned on the water and said, "Let's take a hot, steamy bubble bath instead."

"Sure. That's fine with me, as long as soap and water hit this body. I smell like a bag of onions," I said as I undressed.

"You're still pretty," he said as he undressed.

He was so sexy to me, and I loved the way his thick, pink lips complimented his dark complexion. He sort of reminded me of Taye Diggs. He treated me with so much love and respect. He grabbed my hand as I got in the tub. Then, he got in and sat right behind me. I laid back on his chest, and I felt his dick poking me in my back. It was hard as hell, and it seemed like every time he said a word his dick would move.

"I really did miss you," he said as he splashed bubbles on me. "Did you think about me while you were away?"

"Of course, I did. I thought about you the whole time I was away. I thought about you every single day," he said as he rubbed my back. "I love your beautiful complexion."

He massaged my neck.

"You're very tense," he said as he stroked my body.

"That I am," I said as I let my muscles go and allowed him go to work on my shoulders.

"You have nothing to worry about, baby. I am going to take good care of you."

"That's good to hear," I said as I closed my eyes.

I pictured myself in a wedding dress and imagined that Mama was there, along with Cynthia and Kym, who was there selling her merchandise, as usual. I cracked a smile as I envisioned her getting her hustle on everywhere she went.

"I want to make love to you," Frank said.

After hearing those words, my heart beat fast, and I was at a loss for words. I really wanted to wait until I got my operation, but, since I was going to be his wife, I wanted to make him happy as well.

"I've never done it before," I nervously said.

"I will be gentle," he said as he bathed me. "You are the apple of my eye. I really love you."

"I love you, too," I said as I turned around to kiss him.

We bathed each other, and it was finally time for me to see how it would feel to get fucked in my ass. We made it to the bed, and he dried me off from the bottom of my feet to the top of my head. My hair would always curl up whenever water or steam hit it. He laid me on my back and kissed me and said, "Baby, don't be nervous. I will be gentle and take my time with you."

He laid on the side of me because there was no way that he could lay on top of me since both of our dicks were solid as rocks.

"What do you want me to do for you?" I asked as I continued to kiss him. "Do you want me to suck your dick, or do you want me to fuck you in your ass, too?"

I wanted to see how much he really loved me. I wanted to fuck him in his ass, too.

"You can do both," he said as he stroked his dick.

It looked like it was growing and getting bigger and bigger as he stroked his dick up and down.

"I want to suck your dick," he said as he made his way between my legs.

I was shocked because he didn't appear to be the type. He didn't look like a giver; he looked like a receiver, but Mama had always have told me that looks could be deceiving. And that was the case with him. He sucked my dick fast and slow. He licked up and down the shaft of my dick. My toes curled up, and I felt like I was about to explode in his mouth. He jumped up and said, "Not yet. Don't let loose yet. Let's do the sixty-nine."

"What the hell is the sixty-nine?" I asked, confused.

"It's when two people align themselves, so that each person's mouth is near the other's genitals. I'll show you," he said as he assumed the position. "Wait. You get on top of me since you're light as a feather."

I assumed the position, and his dick was so huge in my mouth. I felt like I was about to choke. *This is fun,* I thought as I slurped up and down his hard dick.

"Do you like that, baby?" he said as he slid one of his fingers into my asshole.

It was uncomfortable, but it kind of felt good at the same time.

"Yes," I said as I felt his teeth nip my dick.

"Ouch," I said as I slowed up my motion on his dick.

"I'm sorry, baby. I am mesmerized by this pretty dick of yours. Are you ready for me to make love to you?"

"Yes," I said as I laid back on the bed. "How do you want it?" I said as I sat up in the bed.

"I want to fuck you in the buck."

"How is that even possible?" I asked as I looked as he walked to get some lubricant.

"Oh, it's possible," he said as he lubed his dick up. "I am going to put both of your legs behind your head. You are limber enough."

I thought he was kidding, but he was dead-ass serious about fucking me in the buck. He twirled my little ass up, and, before I could get a scream out, he had gently slid the head in. Then, he eased his whole dick in.

"How does that feel, baby? Do you like that? Does it hurt?"

"No, it don't hurt, but I feel like I am about to shit on myself."

"That's normal because this is your first time. Ooh, baby! Your ass is so tight. Once I break you in, it will slide in like a slippery snail. Now, I'm about to make love to you. I'm about to put a little more of my dick in. How's that?" he said as he eased more of his dick in my ass.

"It feels good," I said as I relaxed the muscles in my ass.

Then, he stroked faster, and he kissed me. He was

really working up a sweat because sweat was dripping all into my eyes.

My ass was on fire, but I didn't want him to know it. I smiled and continued to lick his sweat.

"I'm about to cum, baby. I'm about fill this pretty, little ass up."

He fucked me harder. Then, I saw a big vein form in the front of his forehead.

I was laying there thinking that there was no way that I could fuck him in his ass. I couldn't even move my hips. He got up, and I watched as his cum fell from his dick to the floor.

"You're looking at a man who hasn't had sex in ages," he said as he caught his breath.

He was breathing hard as he made his way to the sink. He washed up and said, "You don't have to worry about returning the favor. I know that you're a little sore since this was your first time."

I was so relieved when he said that because my asshole was itching and burning at the same time.

28
More Surprises

When I woke up the next morning, I was afraid to move any parts of my body. My ass was still on fire, and I felt like I had to shit. Frank had ordered room service, and I wasn't amused when I saw a huge sausage on the plate.

"I'll pass on the sausage," I said as I poured syrup on my pancakes.

"How do you feel?" he asked as he kissed me on my cheek.

"I feel a bit sore, but I'll live."

"I was gentle with you. I could have been a beast, but I knew to take it easy, considering the circumstances."

He fed me a piece of strawberry off of his plate and said, "I have one more surprise for you."

"More surprises, huh?" I said as I sipped on a glass of orange juice.

"This is the ultimate surprise. We have been living in this suite for quite some time now, and it is time that I treat you like the queen that you are. I bought us a house just up the street from here. It's in Alpharetta."

"You don't have that type of money to go out and buy houses. Do you?"

"Well, at first, I didn't, but I saw an opportunity, and I took it. Let's just say that I, I mean, both of us will never have to work again for the rest of our lives."

"You say that as if you hit the lottery or something."

"I will tell you when the time is right, sweetheart. So,

what I'm about to do is gather all of our things and put them in our car."

I put on my fake breasts. Then, I threw on a dress and headed to the door.

"He said that he accepted me, fake breasts and all," I said to myself as I looked in the mirror.

I was walking slow, and I looked like I had been fucked in my ass. Bob walked over to me.

"I sure am going to miss you, Miss Diana. Whoops! Those weren't there before," he said as he eyed my breasts.

"Well, they're here now, and I am going to miss you, too. Put your tongue back in your mouth, Bob. If your wife needs bigger boobs, then I suggest you buy her some with all of that money I've been spending up in here."

"That's a good idea," he said as he walked away.

Frank pulled to the front of the hotel in a gray Range Rover Sport. I walked around to the back of the truck, and it had more than enough space in the back for all of our luggage from the hotel.

"What's up with the red and blue chains that are on the tires?"

"Those are snow chains. This was the only one like its kind left on the showroom floor, and I had to get it."

He opened the door for me, and I eased onto the smooth cream leather that was trimmed in dark brown. He let the sunroof back, and we rode off and joined the Downtown Atlanta traffic. I looked at my ring, and I said, "This is a big-ass rock."

"It's from the Ross Simons Collection."

"This is a seventy thousand dollar ring!"

"I see you know your diamonds," he said as he held my hand.

"Are you selling drugs? Because, if you are, I am not

going to be involved with a man who is dealing drugs."

"Drugs! Hell, no," he said as he held back a grin.

"Well, how the hell did you buy a Range Rover and a house and a diamond solitaire ring and shit."

"Calm down, sweetheart. I will tell you when the time is right. I am not a drug dealer, and I am not doing anything illegal. Do you believe me? Please trust me and know that I will not put you in harm's way. This house will be our haven, and you don't have to ever leave if you don't want to."

We pulled up at a big house that had what I thought was a never-ending driveway.

"This house looked similar to the one that Mama and I looked at before rained poured on her parade."

"That's okay. Your mama can come here and live with us in this one. It has more than enough room," he said as he opened the door for me.

I was blown away as we entered the house.

This house looked like it was something that celebrities lived in. Then, I thought, *Hell! I am a celebrity*. He had pictures of me on every wall throughout the house, so it wouldn't look so empty.

"How did you get these pictures of me?"

"You don't remember taking pictures at Club Same Attraction?"

"No, I don't, and these are pictures from when I performed in there."

"I thought that this would be something that you would like. Do you want me to take them down?"

"No, of course not. I look like the celebrity I am going to be."

"I will leave the furniture shopping to you," he said as he led me to our master bedroom. "I decorated our bedroom." He turned on the seventy-inch plasma flat screen.

"I love this sleigh bed. My mama had one when I was growing up, and I have always said that this would be what I would get if I ever came across some money."

"This is so nice," I said as I looked around the room and noticed that it looked like we were in Hawaii.

"I like trees, too," he said as he smirked.

"I see," I said as I noticed that they were the same plants that Chris had had delivered in Miami.

I took off of my shoes and laid in the bed. I had so many different thoughts going on in my head. *Nah, he don't know Chris,* I thought as I put a pillow between my legs.

"I am never taking this ring off," I said as I admired it on my hand.

"You're not supposed to. You're going to be my wife soon," he said as he rubbed my feet. "I love this color on your toes. Your feet are gorgeous," He licked across the top of my feet.

He was beginning to creep me out. He was being too damn nice. I wiggled my toes because I wasn't too fond of having my feet licked.

"So, what do you want to do?"

"I want to lay here in this bed for a week until my ass heals."

We both laughed, even though I didn't see shit funny because I was dead-ass serious. *I am never getting fucked in my ass again,* I thought as we watched a Whitney Houston special on television.

29
Frank

After we laid in the bed for almost a month, it really sunk in about what was happening. We had eaten so much pizza that I would have probably thrown up if I saw another pizza commercial on the TV.

My ass had finally healed, and we hadn't had sex ever since. He was definitely being the man of the house. I came to terms with the thought of marriage. This was the life that I had always dreamed of. I had the man of my dreams, and I had a lovely home. And I could dress up whenever I wanted to in my own home without being judged. The thought of us getting married seemed silly. I mean, how could two men marry? But I saw stuff like this on TV all the time. Maybe, it was time for us to be like one of those couples on TV. Frank made sure that I was comfortable in the skin that I was in, but I still wasn't. I had thought deeply about the operation, and we both had agreed to fly out to California to get the procedure done.

We had watched every rerun of *Martin*, and we often compared our relationship to Martin and Gina's. Frank had a great sense of humor, and he kept me laughing. Although he knew that I was an emotional wreck on the inside, he kept my mind off of Mama. He assured me that all things did in fact happen for a reason. He told me that I was still alive for a reason. And that that reason was to follow my dreams. I could be a girl if I wanted, too. And, even though, I was terrified of Daddy, he assured me that he would protect me at all costs, even if it meant losing his life.

I was all alone by myself, so I decided to snoop around the house. This house was so huge that I had to remember my way around this place. Mama had always told me that, if something didn't seem right, I should walk away from it, but this would be hard to walk away from. I went to the detached garage. I knew that something had to be out there. Out of all the houses that I'd ever seen, I'd never seen one with a detached garage. That had instantly raised my suspicion on the first day that we moved in. *This is nice,* I thought as I rubbed the top of a Chevy Camaro.

I walked in, and, to my surprise, I didn't see anything that would make me think that Frank was anyone other than who he claimed to be. There were tools out there and many different lawn mowers. He had pictures of me blown up out there. I was beginning to think that, maybe, he was obsessed with me, but he hadn't shown any irate signs thus far.

When I made it back to the house, he had already made it back.

"Where were you?"

"I was checking out this huge house that sits on three acres. Did you forget that I haven't really had a chance to explore our new home? And I was also admiring that sharp-ass car that you have in that garage out there."

"That was another surprise," he said as his eyes grew big. "That's a Camaro Transformers Special Edition."

"There is something different about you. What is it?" I said as I observed his face very carefully.

"I got my goatee cut off," he said as he felt his chin.

"Wow! You look as young as me now," I said as I walked over and kissed him. "It feels as smooth as a baby's ass." I rubbed my hand on his face.

"I knew you would like it," he said as we went to our

bedroom. "So, what have you been doing since I've been gone? Have you been writing in your diary like I told you to? Writing your feelings down is very therapeutic, especially for someone like you, who has been through so much."

"No, not really. I haven't even thought about that damn diary. I feel like I have been on the run. I feel like I am really in danger from Daddy, and now there is some lunatic bitch that thinks I am sleeping with her man. You're the only man that I am sleeping with, and you promised to God that I am the only one that you're sleeping with. So, who in the hell could this mystery woman be?"

"Maybe, she got the wrong person."

"Maybe, you're right. Maybe, she does have the wrong person, but she seemed so direct in the letter, and she kind of pinpointed things that were right about me."

"Come here, baby. Don't start worrying about nonsense. You see that gun on that dresser? I will blow a motherfucker's head off, if they even act like they want to harm a strand of hair on your head."

I believed him, and, if I was going to transform into a woman, I would need him to be around me twenty-four hours a day.

"Let's go to Cynthia's," I said as I went to my closet to find a gorgeous gown.

I wanted to show that heifer that she was not the only one who could look marvelous. I had to make that bitch eat her words, and I couldn't wait to see the look on her face when she saw me dressed in drag. *She would regret the day that she talked to me like a dog*, I thought as I took a hot bubble bath.

Cynthia had always been jealous of my hair. She didn't get Mama's hair like I did. She got Daddy's looks and his nappy-ass hair. She should have been born a boy, and I should have been born a girl. I looked like a girl, and she had looked like a boy ever since we were kids, but, since she'd had all of that damn plastic surgery done, how could I compete with that? *I should wait and see her after my operation,* I thought as I applied my makeup. *Nah. I will see this bitch today,* I thought as I lined my lips with a nude lip liner.

30
That Bitch Cynthia

I was dressed to kill as I put on a skin tight orange Chanel dress. It had a split up to my thigh, and it showed my long, pretty legs. I made sure I put on two dick tucks so that my big ass dick was well hidden. She was going to be so jealous when she saw me looking like money. I couldn't see why she was so mad at me anyway. She had a big house, and she had married her high school sweetheart. Jayson was the type that would be seen somewhere on the side of the road getting a ticket because he loved to show off his fast cars. He didn't care what the speed limit was. His parents had money, and he had let every government official know that. His parents practically ran Wall Street.

I had to find out myself just how much on the down low that he was. Chris clearly said that Ronnie had been fucking him since the tenth grade. I wondered if Cynthia knew about her so-called perfect husband's boyfriend. He was a fucking faggot, and I would prove it to her.

At first, I was going to be cool with her, until she humiliated me in front of Mama. That was a day that I would never forget. And poor Mama, she just sat there watching her two kids go at it like two crazy people off the streets. Mama had raised us both with manners and values, so we knew better. I still didn't know how I would act when I saw her. I just wanted her to see me when I was dolled up. I wanted her to know that she was not the only one who could look like a pin-up centerfold. She wore Red Bottoms, but I would make sure that she saw me wearing Chris's Rainbow Bottoms. They were much more comfortable and the different colored stripes under the heels were a major plus. I could wear those bad boys with anything. By the time I left her, she would have had a taste of Trey's fever.

I was ready to go, and so was Frank. He had on a black Armani suit with a red shirt and a black brim with a red feather on the side. He, also, had on a pair of Chris's Rainbow Bottom loafers. He looked like a crime lord. He looked like he was down with the mafia.

"You look like a pimp," I said as I watched him put his gun in the holster.

"Are you ready, my sweet thing?" he said as he grabbed his keys off of the dresser.

"I am as ready as I can be. Oh! And I want to drive," I said as I grabbed the keys out of his hand. "This will be a day that that bitch Cynthia will never forget," I mumbled under my breath as we headed for the door.

He turned on the alarm and locked up our house. It still hadn't dawned on me yet that I was living in a mansion. I had so much shit going on right then, and I didn't know whether I was coming or going, but I knew I would feel a lot safer when I saw Daddy in his grave.

I popped the lock on the Range Rover, and Frank, being the perfect gentleman, walked over to the driver's side of the truck and opened the door for me.

"Here you are, my princess," he said as he opened the door.

I adjusted the seat and fixed all the mirrors. Then, I let the sunroof back and turned on the radio. I was listening for Miss Sophia who was on V-103, but I didn't hear her voice, so I changed the station. I liked listening to her. She was so funny to me. I especially loved when she used to do the drum roll with her tongue. She was something fierce on the radio. I couldn't find Miss Sophia, so I put in Gloria Gaynor's "I Will Survive".

All the while, I was listening to the hook. I couldn't think of nothing but surviving Daddy and his crazy-ass ways. I'm not a bad person, and I don't wish no death on nobody but Daddy. He had made my life a living hell for almost twenty years.

Frank was getting in the groove and moving to the song. *He really loves me,* I thought. He was jamming to the rhythm of this song. I took my time and drove the speed limit because I wanted each and every soul to see that I was pushing a new Range Rover. Frank had replaced the snow tires with twenty-four inch Asanti chrome rims. Atlanta was the type of city where everyone wanted to be a celebrity, just because they could wear knockoffs. When I was in high school, I used to look at the girls at my high school, wearing their fake Louis Vuitton and Gucci. I wished I could see them now and let them know that I was wearing the real shit. And I could show them the price tags. I kind of felt bad for not shopping with Kym, but I didn't want any hot clothes. I wanted clothes that were exclusive.

I drove like I was driving Mr. Daisy, considering that Frank was sitting in the passenger seat, looking like an extra from the movie *Hoodlum.*

"I can't wait to meet your sister," he said as he put the song on repeat.

"She's a piece of work," I said as I exited the highway.

"Well, if she's anything like you, I can't wait to meet my new sister-in-law."

Frank had no idea that Cynthia and I didn't get along. I was just merely going over to her place to show her that I was a diva now, too. And he was in for a treat if he thought that I was going to talk nice to her.

When we finally arrived on her street, I slowed down even more, so her sophisticated-ass neighbors could get a glimpse of me. My hair was pulled back in a bun, and the eyelash extensions that I applied were extra long and extra thick. I had also applied rainbow eye shadow that made my Chanel dress stand out. There was nothing anyone could tell me. I looked and felt like a million bucks. I parked the truck next to her Mercedes Benz C-Class, but it didn't have nothing on the Range.

"Stay right there," Frank said as he got out of the truck. "I will open the door for you."

He walked around and opened the door for me. I saw Cynthia and Princess looking at us through her bay windows. When we walked to the door, she opened it wide and welcomed us both in.

"Hey, sis," she sarcastically said as she locked the door behind us.

After Frank took a seat, Princess jumped in his lap. He gently rubbed her head, while I remained standing. I wasn't about to sit down and neither was Cynthia. We just stood there, in the center of her living room, and stared each other down like we were about to wrestle. I observed her from head to toe. She was wearing a white tank top, a pair of LisaRaye fitted jeans and a pair of Red Bottoms. She looked at me from head to toe. First, she looked at the blue contacts that I had in my eyes. Then, she looked at my breasts and smirked. I lifted my leg up a little for her to see the Rainbow Bottoms that I had on. I knew that she was familiar with them because Chris was known nationwide.

"You look good," she said as she hugged me.

"I know I do," I said as I turned around for her to see the booty pad that made me look like I had the perfect ass.

"Too bad all that shit will go up in flames if I strike a match to your ass," she said as she slung her hair out of her face.

She had a razor cut bob, and I knew that she'd had it done by Porsche. It was slanted, and, every time she moved, her hair had so much body and bounce to it.

"And it's too bad that you have to go sit in a salon all day to get your hair done, while I was born with mine."

"Don't forget to add the balls that you were born with," she said as she looked over at Frank.

"Oh, trust me, bitch. He knows all about me. He's a real man. I have a mansion that makes this house looks like a tool shed. I have several cars that I don't have to worry about paying a car note on. I can hop on a plane and go anywhere I want to go, so you can keep all that sassy and smart shit to yourself. And where is your man?" I said as I looked around, after seeing no sign of Jayson. "Did your man finally get tired of listening to you and your bullshit?"

As soon as I said something about Jayson, she instantly changed her tone. She grabbed me by my hand and walked me to her formal dining room. *I did not expect this,* I thought as I sat down. I was enjoying the back and forth confrontation that we'd had going on.

She looked at me with tears in her eyes and said, "Trey, Jayson hasn't been home in over a year. I think something has happened to him."

She was serious, and I felt sorry for her. I never wanted to take jabs at her or make her feel bad, but she was the one who had started this rivalry in the first place. I knew that she needed me now more than ever. Mama was still in a coma, and she needed someone to talk to.

"I am here for you," I said as I put my hand on hers.

"I feel so much better, and that is good to hear coming

from you, considering how I talked to you last time you were here. Trey, I am hurting, and I didn't mean any of those things that I said to you. And what we just said to each other today — let's just squash it."

Then, she stared at her picture of President Obama and Michelle as she reminisced about Jayson and herself.

"I remember when he brought this picture home. We said that we were going to be the bi-racial Michelle and President Obama. In the beginning, he came home every night, and he was even running my bath water. He would add the right amount of oil, and we would make passionate love in my tub. He even cooked for me, making me gourmet meals that I had never even heard of. What the fuck is a Fogo de Chão? And it was so funny to me that he would cook and listen to Diana's Ross's "I'm Coming Out". And, then it was like, he changed overnight. He started going to clubs that I'd never ever heard of. He went to a club called C.S.A. I had never heard that club being advertised on V-103, so I asked Daddy to do some snooping because Jayson wasn't coming home at a decent time like a married man should. He wasn't having sex with me anymore, and he had started verbally abusing me. Can you believe that he had the nerve to ask me if he could fuck me in my ass? I was tired of shopping, and I was tired of being home alone, so I told Daddy that I wanted him to follow Jayson and see what he was up to. And I have never heard from Jayson ever since. I have been getting strange letters, and I have been worrying so much."

I wanted to tell her that her man was on the down low, but that just wasn't the time. I was more interested in the strange letters that she had received.

"Trey, I know that we are not like we were coming up, but I need and love you. You're my only brother. I mean, my only sister," she said as she smiled.

"I love you, too, Cynthia and I never wanted us to have bad blood. I want us to do things together. I love and need you, too," I said as I started to cry.

"Trey, I think that Daddy is behind's Jayson's disappearance."

"When was the last time you talked to Daddy, and, Cynthia, why did Daddy do that terrible thing to Mama?"

"I don't have a clue, but I don't think that Daddy would do that to Mama."

"Oh, yes, he would. I have the proof. He left a letter in the house and told Mama that he would kill us both."

Then, I stopped to think that C.S.A meant *Club Same Attraction*. Jayson was hanging at the same gay club where I was hanging out at.

"Trey, I was all for helping Daddy capture you, but, then, I found out about Mama. And now, Jayson is missing. I don't know what to do."

"What do you mean 'capture me'?" Cynthia, Daddy wants to kill me. There is no simpler way for me to put it."

"Daddy told me that he wanted me to lure you here and then he was going to take you back to Jamaica with him."

"So, you thought that that was okay? Cynthia, look at me. That man does not care for me. If he sliced Mama's throat, he will cut my head off."

"Trey, we need to stick together. Daddy is losing his mind. He cut all his dreads off, and he looks like a bum on the streets, but he is lethal, and no one knows that about him. Trey, Daddy wasn't only a football player. He was in the navy, too, and he knows how to kill with his bare hands. He knows how to survive on the streets. And he is blending in with the bums who roam Downtown Atlanta."

"Well, it would make sense for you to lure him here. Then, we can have Frank kill him."

"Trey, are you suggesting that we kill Daddy?"

"Why not?" I said as I looked at my long, manicured nails. "Look at what he did to our poor old mama. She loved him with every bone in her body. She didn't deserve any of this. If anybody deserves a punishment like that, it's Daddy. He is running around Atlanta looking for me. I saw him one night when I was hanging out at a gay club downtown, but I ran out so fast that I didn't give him a chance to get me. I will not run from him all of my life, though. Cynthia, if you know where he's at, you need to turn him in to the police."

"Trey, you know that our daddy don't give a damn about the police. He's Jamaican for crying out loud."

"You're right," I agreed as I thought back to the letter that she said she had received. "Where is the letter that you received? I want to see it."

"I'll go get it," she said as she walked to her room.

I stared at the picture of President Obama and Michelle. They looked so happy together.

"She is one fine woman," I said as I admired the white gown that she had on.

I was sitting in there, thinking about how I hadn't been able to get dramatic and animated with Cynthia like I had anticipated, but I guessed it wasn't necessary since we had sort of buried the hatchet. I think I'd gotten under her skin. Besides, we looked like twins, so there wasn't too much more that I could say to her.

When she came back, she sat at the table and said, "Be careful. The perfume is funky."

The envelope was just like the one that I had received when I was in Miami. It had no return address, and the handwriting was the same. The fragrance was the same. I opened the letter and it read:

Wrong Man, Wrong Plan

I thought that you were my man and that you had my back,
But you were soft, and I found out where your heart was at.
The men at the bar put you in your place.
Right then and there, I knew that we both needed some space.
You had a side to you that I knew nothing about.
That's why, when that strange man saw you with me, he began to
shout.
I knew something was wrong when you didn't want to kiss me,
And I opened my eyes, and I began to see
That you didn't want a "she"; you wanted a "he",
And our love could never be meant to be.
I thought that it was me, but it wasn't my fault.
Now, my heart is locked away from all other men like a vault.
I don't even know which man that I can trust.
You hurt me so bad, now all I want to do is go out and lust.
How could you do this to me? How could you do this to us?
On the day we met, I should have had more to discuss.
You didn't have to prove to me and act like a man
Because you were the wrong man with the wrong plan.
I saw all of the signs, but I just couldn't believe
That you had this shady low down shit under your sleeve,
But you didn't look gay, nor did you act gay.
It was something that made you that way.
I don't have anything against them because that's what they do,
But you were my man and my heart was all into you,
And what about our son that I gave birth to last year?
Well, I won't ever allow you to come near.
I see you when you're acting as happy as can be,
But did he tell you that we were both HIV?

31
Shocked

I was so shocked after I read that letter. My mouth was literally on her marble floor.

"Oh, my God! Have you been tested for HIV? Who have you been sleeping with?"

"Trey, you know that Jayson was my one and only. He was my first and my last. And, yes, I have been tested, and I am HIV positive."

I put my hands over my mouth and wept like a little child.

"Please don't cry. I have cried enough about this already, and I have prayed about this. My life is in God's hands now. There's nothing that anyone can do about my HIV status."

"Cynthia! Cynthia! Cynthia, why wasn't that the first thing that you told me when I walked through your front door?"

"Because I knew that you had some anger to get out because of how we ended our visit last time."

"This is so serious. Did you know that you were HIV positive back then?"

"Of course, I knew. Why do you think I fired off at you like that? I went and had all of this surgery done, trying to use up all of Jayson's money, but his parents are tycoons, and the money just keeps on growing. They didn't even care when I told them that he hadn't been home in over a year. Don't worry about me, Trey. I can live with HIV. I go to the doctor once every three months, and, each time I go, he tells me that all I have to do is have the willpower and desire to live. My T-cell count is very high, so that means, if I went and took an HIV test right now, it would probably come back negative. So I take the doctor's advice; I eat right, and I exercise, and I do plenty of praying. You know I got that praying from Mama. Do you remember how we used to say our prayers when we were kids? You would say at the end of every prayer, 'Thank you, Jesus, for my long hair.' And Mama and I would bust out laughing at you. I still find that funny. Believe it or not, those good memories are what have kept me so strong, especially when I think about all of the stuff that you and I have been through."

"I can't believe how well you're taking this," I said as I put the letter back in the envelope.

"What can I do? What's done is done? And I wouldn't change nothing in my life because all I did was love one man. I was faithful to him. I loved him. And look at what happened to me. I got the shitty end of the stick, but I have strong faith in God, and I know that He will never forsake me."

"I feel so bad for you, though. You don't deserve this type of treatment."

I sat there, wondering if I should tell her that Jayson was fucking my teacher, but, like she had said, there was nothing that anyone could do. *So I will just keep it to myself for now*, I thought.

When we both heard Princess bark, I said, "Honey child, I forgot all about Frank."

We walked to the front room and found that Frank had dozed off on the sofa. Princess was at the door. She was house trained, and she knew when it was time for her to go. Cynthia let Princess outside, and I tapped Frank on his knee, waking him up.

He woke up and stretched and said, "Are you ready to go, baby?"

"Not yet. I want to introduce you to my sister Cynthia. Cynthia, this is my good man Frank. He asked me to marry him. Look at this rock," I said as I held my hand up.

"I saw that when you first walked through that door. That's from the Ross Simons Collection, isn't it? You know that I know my diamonds." She looked at Frank and said, "It's nice to meet you. Please take good care of my sister."

He shook her hand and said, "The pleasure's all mine, and I will take very good care of Trey."

She looked at me and said, "Trey, I am really happy for you. I am glad that all of your dreams are finally coming true."

"Frank, can you wait for me in the truck? I will be out in just a second. I want to say my good-byes to my sister in private."

"Sure," he said as he opened the door.

Princess came flying in, and she hopped on the sofa.

"Cynthia, we have to stick together more than ever now because all we have is each other. I mean, we have Auntie Barbara and Kym, but they are useless."

"You're right about that because the judge has thrown the book at Kym. And Auntie Barbara is going crazy raising all those bad-ass kids. Can you believe she had the nerve to ask me if I wanted two of them? I thought about it, but I have my own problems. Plus, Princess and I have gotten used to living here alone."

"What do you mean 'the judge has thrown the book at her'?"

"She's in jail for stealing all of that Gucci and Prada shit. I told that girl that she could have gotten an honest nine to five, but she wasn't hearing that. She was used to that fast easy money. Now, she has to do fifteen years of hard time. I talk to her from time to time. I get collect calls on my phone, so I can talk to her. She told me that she saw you singing in drag in Miami. I wish I could have seen you. You always could sing your little heart out," she said as she closed her bay window curtains.

"You would have wanted to see me?"

"Of course, I would have loved to have seen you. Why wouldn't I? At least, one of our dreams have come true. It figures it would be yours."

"My dreams won't come true as long as Daddy is breathing. That's why you and I have to come up with a plan to kill him."

"Trey, I don't want us to go to jail like the Menendez Brothers."

"You're right. I don't want to go to jail either. I didn't quite think that one through," I said as I fidgeted with the ring on my finger. "We could never get away with murder. I could see us now on *The First 48*, and I would be the first to rat you out."

"I know you would because I am the strong one," she said. "I will think of a plan to get Daddy to say that he tried to kill Mama, and maybe that will put him away for a little while. I will call you as soon as I come up with a plan."

She hugged me. Then, I left.

32
Frank the Hitman

"I was just about to come in and get you," Frank said as I walked out to the truck.

"You can drive," I said. "I don't want to shine anymore."

"What's wrong, baby? Is everything alright?"

"Yes, everything is okay."

"What's the rush with you?"

"I am not in a rush. I just have a meeting that I need to attend."

"Let me guess. You will tell me when the time is right."

"You are so right," he said as he backed out of Cynthia's driveway.

She was looking at us, once again, through her big, pretty bay windows, and we both waved good-bye to each other. I felt so bad for her. How could she live with herself knowing that she had HIV? But she said that she could live a long time with it. And I believed her because I had seen an HIV special on TV, and one of the people that were featured had been living with full blown AIDS for almost twenty-eight years. And that was because he had the will to live. I believed Cynthia when she said that she wanted to live a long, productive life. I pulled my diary out and wrote about my sister Cynthia.

Dear Diary,

Well, today didn't go quite like I had planned. I wanted Cynthia's face to hit the floor when she saw me looking as good as her, but, when she told me her bad news, my mouth was damn near on the floor. Now, I am starting to think that, since we both received the same letters, maybe I should go get checked for HIV, but I haven't been fucking nobody but Chris, and no one has been fucking me but Frank. He hasn't shown me any signs of there being another woman. He has taken me all over town, and no one seems to want to out him or anything. And, if Ronnie is the one writing the letters, why would he portray himself as a woman? It just doesn't make sense.

Could it be Daddy writing these letters? Nah, if Daddy had been that close to me in Miami, I would be dead by now. Well, who in the hell could it be? I am at a loss for words right now. Maybe, it's a crazy bitch that has our identities mixed up, but she couldn't be wrong because Cynthia is HIV positive.

Ugh!!! What should I do? I see why they say cherish your mama while she's living, and, even though Mama isn't dead, it sure seems like she is. I can't talk to her, and now is a time that I could really use her expertise. She could fix this if she had the strength. Or did Cynthia and I put ourselves in this position? Is Cynthia lying? Did she cheat and give Jayson HIV? Is that why he ran away? I don't know what to think, but I do know that I will stay at home for a while, especially since Jayson hung out at Club Same Attraction.

Should I dig deep into Frank's past? How do I know that he is who he says he is? He could have a wife and kids hidden somewhere, and I would never know. He told me that he was from Philly. What if they are there? What if he has a whole different family? What if he is the man that she's talking about in the letter? That can't be true because Cynthia would have said something, or would she? I am starting to get beside myself, thinking all sorts of outrageous things. She just spilled her heart out to me, and I know that she wouldn't keep it a secret from me if she was in fact sleeping with Frank. How would I know? They both seemed to not know one another, or did they?

Damn it, Diary. I don't know what to think! Who could this mysterious woman be? Who is behind these hideous-ass letters? A real bitch would reveal herself. Whoever she is, she's pissed off because her down low ass man gave her HIV. Wait a minute! What if Cynthia's the one who is behind the letters? What if everything that she told me was a big, fat, black lie? I have to really put my thinking cap on, and, when I was talking to her, I wasn't too fond of hearing her say that she was going to help Daddy capture me. What the fuck is that all about? That shit sounds illegal. Terrorists get captured. Not a damn American citizen. Maybe, she is trying to butter me up and set me up for Daddy to get me. While she is coming up with a plan, I will be coming up with one as well. She had so much hate in her eyes when we argued the last time. So how could she change soft all of a sudden? I actually enjoyed having someone to hate, but, since she has turned the tables, I have to switch back to nice mode. I won't let my guard all the way down. Mama didn't raise no fool. I won't be a fly in her and Daddy's web.
The End

"I'm going to stop right here and grab a bite to eat," Frank said as we pulled into a burger joint.

"I don't want nothing to eat; I can't eat right now."

"Are you sure? These are the best burgers in the world."

"I'm sure," I said as I looked around at our surroundings.

He went in to get himself something to eat. I tried to open the glove compartment, but I was shit out of luck because it was locked. I was reaching on the side of the doors while I kept my eyes on him as he stood in line.

"Shit! Nothing," I said as I sat back in the truck. I looked around the truck, and it was clean as a whistle. There was nothing in there out of place.

"What is his car doing here?" I said as I looked at a car that looked similar to Chris's red Benz.

I lowered my long body down in the truck.

"Is it just a coincidence that Frank wants to stop here and that Chris is here?"

I watched Chris as he twisted and got in his car. "That short lying bastard! If he knows Frank, I will give him a piece of my mind. I will kill him!"

Frank got back in the truck, after putting his food in the back on the floor.

"Baby, did you see that billionaire in there? He is the designer of these shoes that we are wearing. I think his name is Rainbow Chris or something like that," he said as he pulled off.

"No, I didn't see him, I was out here with my eyes closed, listening to 'I Will Survive'," I lied because I was not stupid.

I had to find out if those two knew each other. And, if they did, what connection did they have? Kym did say that, when Daddy attacked Mama, he was in a red Benz. She said that he was going so fast that she had got a speeding ticket trying to catch him. There weren't too many people riding around Atlanta in a red Benz like his, so, now, I needed to find out if it Daddy who was in Chris's Benz.

I was starting to get knots in my stomach. I didn't know who to trust. My life was starting to crumble. It seemed like I was putting the pieces together with the few people that I had in my circle. I couldn't put them together, but they all seemed affiliated somehow. And for Frank to pull up at that burger joint and for Chris to be there....that was not a coincidence. I was young, but I wasn't dumb. I was around people who had money, and money could buy a lot of shit, including tombstones. Daddy probably had Mama's lottery ticket. What if he was paying Cynthia to set me up? If Jayson was dead or gone, I was sure that they had stopped the funds in his bank account. I was starting to put the pieces to the puzzle together. *Now that I think of it Cynthia was crying crocodile tears. I was the one who was weeping like Little Bo Peep. That slick bitch,* I thought as I took off my seatbelt. We were at home, and I let myself out of the truck.

"I got it," I said as Frank was about to walk to the passenger's side.

"Well, let me walk you in and make sure everything is cool."

"Why wouldn't everything be cool?" I asked as I looked around.

"I know everything is cool. It's just you have been on edge lately, and I want to make sure that you get in safely."

He walked me to the door, and I locked the door behind him and turned on the alarm. I turned on every light on the lower level of the house. *How do the rich and lonely live in big-ass houses all by themselves?* I thought.

I went to the computer and did a name search on Franklin Benjamin in Philadelphia's data base. And his picture popped up on the FBI's Most Wanted List.

"What the fuck?" I said as I stepped back from the computer.

He was wanted for several murder for hire jobs all over America. I heard the door open. Then, the lights went off.

"Shit!" I said as I went to go hide in the pantry in the kitchen. "He's coming back to kill me," I said as I closed the pantry door.

Then, I heard a voice say, "Come out, come out, wherever you are!"

It was Frank.

I came out of the pantry, and I said, "Why did you turn off of the lights? And how did you change clothes that quick?"

He didn't say anything. He grabbed me by my hair and threw me on the floor.

"Frank, why are you doing this to me? You asked me to marry you, remember?"

He had a long silver gun, and he rolled a silencer on the end. He pointed the gun at me, and I had a flashback of when Chris and Ronnie played that prank on me, but this was real. He grabbed me by my hair and pushed me to the floor.

"Frank, please don't kill me. Whatever my daddy is paying you, I can double that."

He put the gun to my temple, and I heard a loud bang, but I was still alive. Frank fell on top of me and blood was all over the kitchen floor.

"Baby, are you okay?" It was Frank.

"Hell, no! I'm not okay. You just tried to kill me."

"That was my twin brother, and he was hired by your daddy."

"How do I know that you are who you say you are?"

He turned his brother onto his back and opened his shirt. He had HIT MAN tattooed on his chest.

"You saved my life once again," I said as I ran into his arms.

"I told you to call me your guardian angel. I see that you don't believe what I told you. I see that you have been doing your homework on the computer."

"But how did you know that he would come for me?"

"As I was leaving, I saw the motion light come on by the detached garage, so I hurried back for you. I didn't know that he would go this far, but we were like oil and water coming up. He was always the macho man, and I was a mama's boy."

"Well, why didn't you ever mention that you had a twin?"

"Because, for me, he died a long time ago. I am going to go bury him in the back."

"No, the fuck you're not! I am not going to live in this house knowing that your dead twin is buried in the back."

He put his gun in his holster, and he got on the phone and dialed 911. I got on the computer and found a biodegradable cleaning crew. Then, we called the FBI, who were very adamant about their reward. Frank's brother was wanted dead or alive, and the reward was two million dollars. The uniformed cops didn't show up; the real FBI showed up in suits and long trench coats.

The first one walked in the door and said, "That's him alright. Fredrick "The Hit Man" Benjamin."

"It sure as hell is," the other agent said.

"Here's your fifty dollars."

One agent had bet the other that it would not be him. Before the agent left, he looked at Frank and said, "Everybody at the Bureau thought that it would be your sweet ass, lying in the middle of the floor with a bullet in your head."

33
Sensitive Frank

Frank and I never really spoke about the night that he killed his own brother. All he kept saying was that his brother was full of evil. I still had a lot of unanswered questions floating around in my head, but being alive was enough for me. We both stayed in the house every single day for about three months. He even kept a diary. He didn't hide it from me. He let me read it.

Frank's Diary

Dear God,

I know that it's been a while since we talked, but you see everything and you already know what a brother has been going through. Even though I am living in sin, I try to do the right thing. I know that I was raised in the church, but, ever since Pastor Pickle used to play with my dick in Sunday school, I never really had any interest in women. I mean, you know that I have had a couple of girlfriends here and a couple of girlfriends there, but, God, you know my heart, and my heart wants to be with the same sex. Mama would be so proud of me if she could see me now. She knew the real me, and she never judged me.

She wouldn't be happy that I had to kill her other son, but it was either him or my man. She had always told me that Fredrick's soul was cold. She said that he used to watch a lot of gangster movies when he was younger. He would watch movies such as <u>Scarface</u>,

<u>The Godfather</u>, <u>Casino</u> and <u>Heat</u>. She said that he was infatuated with guns and that he hadn't been right since she'd sent him off to boarding school. I hardly ever saw him when we were younger because he was always in trouble, but Mama had done her best with him. She really did, but some seeds were just born bad, and there was no changing them. And it's sad to say that my brother was born a bad seed. She did what she thought was best for her family. Daddy was never around. She didn't talk about him, and we didn't ask about him either. As far as I was concerned, she was our mama and our daddy. She raised me good, and, because of her, I know how to be a good man. She taught me how to love, and now I am in love with Trey. He's young, innocent and very smart. He's a bit snappy, but I can handle that. I love him for who he is. He's not afraid of a challenge, and, for him, that challenge is his life. And it doesn't matter if he has the surgery or not, I will love him no matter what.

I know you probably frowned down on me when I had to shoot my brother in the back of his head, but I had no choice. He was about to shoot the love of my life. I am so glad that you finally sent me someone who understands and loves me. He doesn't judge me, and I don't judge him. We're perfect together. I know that it was you who placed him at Club Same Attraction. And I want to thank you for that. They say that there is somebody for everybody. Trey is that somebody for me. I love him with all of my heart, and I will do all I can to see that smile of his brighten up my every day, even if it means killing his daddy. I killed once, and I will kill again. Even though I am a homosexual, I am still a man first. And that means I will protect my family to the fullest. I love Trey so much. I love how he sleeps with a pillow under his legs. I love it when he smacks his lips and snaps his fingers. I love everything about him. I love it when we go out to eat, and he rolls his neck when he places his order. When we go out, I see how the women stare at us. I feel how they look at us like we don't belong, but, God, we're your people, too, and only you can judge us. I am so glad that Mama taught me to humble myself because I can take all kinds of criticism. Some women can be so mean, though. I mean there have been times that they have walked up to us and said to me, "You look too good to be getting fucked in your ass." And little do they know that I've never been fucked in my ass. It's just a damn shame that there are so many desperate women out there, who can't get a man to save their lives, but women like them make me put Trey on a pedestal. I want to thank you again for uniting us because we're a match made in heaven. The End.

I had tears in my eyes after I finished reading his diary. *He really does love me*, I thought as I closed his diary. If that wasn't love and loyalty, then I didn't know what was. I hated to hear that he had been molested as a young boy. And out of all places, it took place at the damn church. I didn't know what to believe. I didn't know if I should follow Allah or Jesus Christ. Religion was just so confusing, so all I did was pray. I didn't like going to church because I hated all those evil looks that the goody two shoes Christians gave me, so I had my own personal relationship with God, and he'd been with me thus far. I couldn't believe that Frank had never been fucked in his ass. *Maybe, I won't have the operation after all. Maybe, I will satisfy him just how he satisfies me*, I thought. Well, he didn't exactly satisfy me because I had been in excruciating pain, but some of the pain was good, and, overall, I enjoyed looking at his sexy-ass chest and his six pack. I looked over at him on the bed, and he didn't have on nothing but a pair of black silk boxers.

"So, did you enjoy reading my diary?" he asked as he made room for me to lay next to him.

"I sure did. I enjoyed each and every detail. I'm sorry to hear that you were molested."

"Baby, don't feel sorry for me. That only made me a stronger man for you."

"So, am I your first same sex relationship?"

"Actually you are. I had kept myself so busy with work. I had women to try and holler at me, but women just weren't my cup of tea. Now, I'm not going to sit up here and lie. I got a couple of phone numbers, but it was only to chat. I didn't want to mislead them in any way. I know where my heart is, and it's right here with you. I knew that you were going to be mine the same night that I met you. I saw that twinkle in your eye. And, even though you were just a kid back then, I knew that I had to protect you. You are what I have been looking for all of my life. I want you to make love to me," he said as I kissed his thick lips.

"Are you afraid that my big dick will hurt you?" I joked.

"No, I'm not afraid," he said as he grabbed me and put his tongue in my mouth.

Both of our dicks were rock hard. I went to the dresser to get the lubricant.

"You don't need that," he said as he went down and sucked on my dick.

"Are you sure? You don't have to play Randy 'Macho Man' Savage with me. I understand if you want me to lube my dick up."

"No need for lube. My saliva is just as thick, so, after I suck it, it will be dripping wet, and all you have to do is slide it in my ass. So you remember how I eased a little of my head in, then I began to stroke slowly? That's what I want you to do."

After he was done sucking my dick, it was sloppy wet, just like he had said it would be.

"I don't want to fuck you in the buck. I want to fuck

you from the back."

There was just something about that for me. I liked to see the muscles in a man's back. He bent over, and I eased the head in slowly. Then, I stroked just like he had told me to do. He was moaning my name as he took all of my big-ass dick.

"Yeah, Trey! Just like that," he said over and over.

I watched my dick go in and out, and it was a good look to me. I was feeling that feeling, but I wasn't ready to come. I wanted it to last. *How come orgasms can't last for a whole hour? They are the best damn feelings in the world.*

He was throwing his ass back, and I couldn't help it. I came all in his ass. I rested my chest on his back as we both fell down on the bed.

"That was good, baby," he said as he wiped sweat from my face.

"Now, I see why you were sweating when you were making love to me. That's a job back there," I said as I laid on my side of the bed. "Are you sore? Did I hurt you?"

"I am a little sore, but I will live. That felt good, baby, and I want you to do it again and again. I will never get tired of you."

He went to go draw us a hot, steamy bubble bath. He didn't even walk like he was in pain, like I did my first time. *Maybe, since he's older, his muscles are stronger than mine*, I thought.

We did our normal routine when we took a bath together. We bathed each other, and I laid back on him, talking to him about whatever came to mind. We both knew how to communicate, and that was a plus for our relationship.

After we got out of the tub, I went to the kitchen and whipped us up a meal. We both had worked up an appetite. I was a quick learner, and I watched him as he prepared our meals. I fixed us some butterfly grilled shrimp, rice pilaf and mixed veggies.

34
Life Goes on

Life went on despite knowing that Daddy was out to kill me. Life continued on despite knowing that Mama was still in the hospital. I really wanted to visit her, but how? Frank had assured me that he would go with me and that he would protect me if Daddy showed up and showed out.

I really missed Mama. I missed her cooking, and I missed that pretty smile of hers. I really missed all of the love and advice that she would have for me every time that she saw me. It didn't matter if I wanted to hear it or not, she would give it because those were just her motherly instincts. I couldn't remember the exact number of times she had taken up for me when Daddy wanted to kill me, but I knew it was a lot. She was such a good mama, and I wished that there was some way that I could go visit her.

Frank and I had been spending so much time together that we were inseparable. He loved me just as much as I loved him. We still hadn't gotten married, but that would take place soon after my surgery. There was no way that I would be getting married in snap-ons and add-ons on my wedding day. When Mama married Daddy, she looked like a diva, and, when Cynthia married Jayson, she looked like a diva as well, so why not keep it in the family?

When I went to Cynthia's house and saw her and Jayson's wedding picture. She appeared to be the happiest woman in the world in that photograph, but she was hurting deep down inside. That was why she spent unnecessary money on dog collars and thousand dollar ferns. Even though she had tried to be big and bad when I was over there, I had seen right through all of that plastic surgery, but I couldn't understand why was she so furious at me. We had been thick as thieves growing up. Then, all of a sudden, she flipped the script on me. I really missed how we used to talk out our problems, but now it was like a screaming match whenever we saw each other. I missed all the times that she used to play in my hair. I missed all the times when we used to play school. I was really feeling kind of bad, and I didn't even know why. I hadn't changed; she had changed, and for what? I had yet to find out why she was so bitter towards me. We didn't start feuding until we got older. After high school, she immediately moved in with Jayson, and I didn't see any signs of her disliking me. As far as I was concerned, we were still cooler than a fan. Then, she flipped out when I visited her with Mama. I thought that she would have been happy to see me, but, boy, was I wrong. She was so mad, and I saw it in her eyes. She had Daddy's eyes, and I saw him in her when she talked to me like a dog.

Frank was out and about, and he told me that I could read his diary any time I felt like it. I hadn't written in mine in a minute, but I was eager to see what he had in his because he wrote in his diary quite often. I was glad that he was out. Even though he said that I could read it anytime, I didn't feel right reading it in front of him. I wondered to his side of the bed and reached under the mattress and grabbed his diary. Frank's diary read:

Daddy wasn't there.
You're a man that I will never forget.
You left because you couldn't help Mama pay half on the rent.
You didn't even have money to feed your two sons,

And Mama said that you'd became a fugitive and on the run.
Out of sight is never out of mind,
Especially if that person is in your mind.
I remember you so much,
But it hurts my heart that you didn't keep in touch.
Mama was there for us no matter what,
Even when she had to put the belt to our butts.
She raised us to the best of her knowledge,
And guess what! We both went to college,
But somehow Frederick ended up with a bitter rage,
And he should have been locked in a cage.
I didn't want to kill my own twin brother,
But I was looking for a choice and had no other.
Do you see what happens when a man leaves home?
Some kids go haywire and turn out all wrong,
But only one of us turned out to be violent and bad,
And I had to put a bullet in his head, and I was so sad.
Daddy, we both just needed your love and touch,
But Mama made sure that she loved us a whole bunch.
Boys will be boys, but that's not always true.
We needed someone, and that someone was you.
I am a man who's living with a man,
But this is my life and my plan.
If you were there, I'd probably still be gay,
And it's because I just love being this way.
I love being with another man, and we have so much fun,
Even though he is living on the run.
We love each other, and that's all that matters,
And, if something ever happened to Trey, my heart would shatter.

     I wonder if I should tell Trey that I am being paid to keep him alive, but he's going to read my diary anyway, so it's better if he finds out this way. He probably won't understand me. Hell! He probably won't even believe me. It's no accident that I was at the club the night that he needed to be rescued from his daddy. His daddy paid me to kill him, and Chris had paid me to keep him alive. It was just business at first, but the more time I spent with him, the more I fell in love with him. I remember like it was yesterday. Trey's dad had come up to me at the club and said that he wanted it to be done that same night. He walked up to me and just started talking to me out of nowhere. And I knew that he had me confused with my twin brother once he had given me a picture of Trey. I played along with his game, and I said that I had needed more money. He said that he had just given Frederick ten million dollars. I told him that the price had doubled, so he gave me ten million dollars that night. Then, out of nowhere, this short, white man came up to me, and he was damn near out of breath.

He said, "I know that someone is paying you to kill someone, but I will pay you to keep him alive."

Then, he started saying that he was going to go along with Trey's daddy's plan. But he said that he didn't want to live the rest of his life in jail. He told me that he was Chris "The Rainbow" Hyatt. I knew that he looked familiar, but I couldn't pinpoint where I knew him from. He was the famous designer, and he was famous for his Rainbow Bottom shoes, but, when I first met Trey, he was so innocent and scared that there was no way that I could tell him all of this. His daddy wanted him dead, and his own good friend had betrayed him, so I saw an opportunity, and I took it. Chris gave me fifty million dollars in cash. I had so much money, and I could have killed him and moved out of the country, but I loved him, and there was no way that I could hurt him. All I can do is stall Trey's daddy by telling him that the time just isn't right. His daddy is one crazy son of a bitch. He wants me to fuck Trey in his ass before I kill him. And he wants me to videotape his murder. I am working on recording Trey's daddy, so I can have him put away for good. He needs to be locked up behind bars.

35
Who do I Trust?

I was in complete shock when I closed Frank's diary.

"How could he keep such a horrible secret from me? And, to make matters worse, he's keeping in contact with my crazy-ass daddy! What should I do? I should leave here, but where can I go? I can't trust anyone. Cynthia hates me, and Chris is in on the plot to kill me," I said as I paced around the room.

Suddenly, I knew who I could call. I could call Ronnie, but what if he found out that I had fucked Chris on numerous occasions. This was bad, so damn bad! I had no one to run to.

I grabbed a few of my things and headed to the detachable garage, but, to my surprise, the car was gone. Now, I was really getting scared. I was in the middle of nowhere, and my closest neighbors were a mile away. I would just have to hitchhike and get myself a hotel room downtown again. At least, Bob made sure that no one came up to my room. As I headed down our driveway, I saw Frank in the Camaro.

"Where are you going?" he asked as he stopped the car.

"What do you care?" I yelled as I kept walking.

"Trey, will you please stop and let me talk to you? What is wrong with you?" he said as he grabbed my hand. "Where are you going with these bags?"

I looked him in his eyes, and I started to cry because I trusted him so much.

"I am leaving because I read your diary, and you know more than you've told me."

"I didn't hide anything from you. And I am glad that you read my diary. Trey, if I wanted to kill you, I could have been did it by now. I love you. Can't you see that? I am putting a plan together that will put your psycho daddy away forever. Trey, will you stop walking and talk to me?"

He was looking so handsome when I stared into his eyes.

"Why should I believe you?"

"Trey, look at me," he said as he turned my face to look back at him again. "I am not the bad guy here. I want us to have a future together. I didn't tell you all of that stuff because I didn't want you to think that I was on their side."

"Well, weren't you on their side at first?"

"No, I was never on their side. The opportunity was just so sweet, and the plan was for me to record your daddy, but he is so damn smart that he searches me at every meeting. I was going to fool him today, but he didn't show up. Please, at least, come back to the car with me and let me show you all of the small high tech security cameras that I went out and bought."

I believed him, so I walked towards the car. We both got in the car, and he turned to me and said, "This will do it for me."

He pulled out a pair of shades.

"How in the hell are a pair of shades going to get Daddy arrested?"

"That's the beauty of it," he said as he showed me the frame of the shades. "This is where the camera is. Right here. Here. Look in the back," he said as a TV screen came on. "This is all hooked up together, and this is how I will get your daddy. For some odd reason, your daddy wasn't there today. He's never not shown up for a meeting, but I wanted to be the one who eventually put your daddy away."

"What if he's coming to kill me himself? What if he comes to our house?"

"Trey, that's nonsense. He has no idea where we live."

We got out of the car and went into the house. I still had a lot more questions for him. He was not getting off the hook that easy. When we walked into our bedroom, I didn't have to start the conversation off. He had already had the feeling that he had more explaining to do.

He sat next to me on the bed and said, "I am so sorry for keeping this secret from you. I know what type of man your daddy is, and I wanted to protect you from him myself. I went out and spent high dollars on all of that equipment in the car."

"It's not like you couldn't afford it," I said as I rolled my eyes at him.

"But you should be happy for us. I was going to tell you about the money. Why do you think you can afford everything that you lay your pretty eyes on? I made that possible, and I know I was wrong for not telling you, but you already had enough on your plate."

"Are there anymore secrets that you're hiding from me?"

"No, of course not. You have my heart in your hands," he said as he kissed the top of my hand. "I even know about you and Chris, but I'm not jealous or mad. I figured that you were probably in a compromising position, and you had to do what you had to do. So, now can we just move on and put the past behind us. How does a trip to Vegas sound?"

"We can go to Vegas after I recover from my surgery. I am ready to be a woman."

"You're still serious about that?"

"Why wouldn't I be?" I said as I removed my hand from his. "Will you be ashamed of me or something?"

"Of course not. I just don't want that big-ass dick you have to get chopped off and go to waste. I love it when we make love. I love it when you make me scream your name."

"I don't know if I can take it in my ass anymore," I said as I felt my butt.

"Baby, that was because it was your first time, I promise it won't hurt anymore."

"Why are you looking at me like you want to have sex right now," I said as I rolled my neck at him.

"Because I do want to make love to you at this very second. And I want you to make love to me, too. How does that sound?" he said as he laid me on my back and kissed me. "I want you to trust me and know that I am not out to hurt you."

He unbuttoned his fitted Levi's jeans.

"How could I say no to you?" I said as I took off of my clothes.

We were just about to begin our passionate lovemaking when, all of a sudden, our alarm went off. We both jumped up and ran downstairs only to discover that someone had thrown a brick through our window with an envelope that read YOU HAVE BEEN WARNED!

36
You've Been Warned

I felt weak in the knees when I opened up the letter. Frank ran outside to see if he could see anyone, but they had already left. This letter was just like all the rest of them. It, also, had the stench of that same fragrance. I opened it up and read it silently. When Frank sat beside me on the sofa, I fixed my lips and read it out loud.

You've been warned.
And, yes, I am a woman that has been scorned.
I see you flaunting in the streets in your Rainbows.
I have the ups on you, and you don't even know.
I can get to you whenever I want to,
And that's just it. I am coming for you.
I am tired of being the stressed out wife.
So, why won't you just get out of my life?
My man loves me even when he's with you.
I've given you plenty of time for your relationship to be through.
I am ten steps ahead of you.
As you can see,
I want my man back at home with me.
At first, it was supposed to be all fun and games,
But he has fallen in love with you, and I am to blame.
I went along with his plan, and it has somehow backfired.
Now, enough of this shit. I am getting tired.
I will reveal myself to you when the time is right,
And I won't leave without putting up a fight,

So do yourself a favor, and leave my man alone.
He needs to come back to me and live at our home.
I am tired of raising our kids on my own
Because with me is where he belongs!

After I read the letter, I looked at Frank's body language. This has to be in reference to him. I was not sleeping with no one else but him. *I am not stupid,* I thought as I balled the letter up.

"Frank, will you be honest with me for once?" I said as I threw the letter at him.

"Baby, I am being honest with you. I am with you, and I am in love with you. I hold your hand when we go out on the town."

He did have a point, but who could these mysterious letters be coming from? I was so confused. We had been together for a long time, and I really believed him. So, now, I was back at square one— confused as fuck! He came over and held my hand.

Then, he looked in my eyes and said, "You don't have anything to worry about. I am in love with you and only you. Now, can we finish what we started?"

He kissed me on my neck. "I've already called a repairman to come and fix the window. He will be here later this evening."

"Frank, I know that you say your heart is in the right place, but I can't make love right now. Maybe later, but, right now, I want you to call Daddy and find out where he is because I have to see Mama."

"It's not that easy. I usually wait for him to call me. I will make sure I am ready to put his ass in jail for good, but I promise you. My plan will work because, once I get him on tape for attempted murder of your mama, he will be gone for a very long time, if not for the rest of his life. And I also have some news about Jayson."

"How do you know Jayson?" I said as my heart skipped a beat.

"I know all about his relationship with Ronnie."

"You know Ronnie, too?" I said as I looked at him with a mean mug on my face. "I asked you to be honest with me, Frank, so, when were you going to tell me that you knew my sister's husband? Have you fucked him?"

"No, I haven't slept with him. Your daddy filled me in on everything. He told me that he hated gays with a passion. He said that your sister had told him about Jayson's behavior. She told him that she wanted your daddy to follow him and see what he was up to. He told me that he followed him to some cabins in Tennessee. He said that they were fucking and he said that he tried to stay awake. He said that he wanted to kill them both."

"What do you mean? Are you trying to say that Jayson is dead?"

"Let me finish telling you the story. He said that he was so tired from that long drive. He said that he fell asleep, and, when he woke up, he found Jayson sound asleep. He said that he crept in and strangled him and put him in the trunk. He said that it was his body at your house. Jayson's parents didn't find out until later last year. They had gotten a tip from an anonymous caller. He wanted the authorities to think it was him, so he could get away with murder."

"So wait a minute. Back up. You mean to tell me that you were with me at my sister's house, and you didn't think to tell her that her man was dead? What kind of person are you? So you haven't been completely honest with me?"

"I have been protecting you," he said as sweat started to flow down his face.

"Look at me, Trey. I am here for you, and I will make sure that you live your dream. I am here to make sure that you are happy. When your daddy stressed to me that he hated gays with a passion, I knew that I couldn't go along with his plan."

"Does Daddy know that you're gay?"

"Of course not, but this isn't about me. This is about us putting his crazy ass away for good."

"So, I guess the money you're spending is Mama's money."

"I don't know anything about that. All I know is that he came to me with a sweet deal."

"Frank, Mama hit the lottery, and Daddy stole it and set the house on fire."

"Well, I guess it is hers then, but we have plenty of money left. When your mama gets better, she can come here and live with us."

"I have one more question for you," I said as I held his hand. "Do you know my sister Cynthia?"

"No, I do not know your sister. No, I am not cheating on you."

"I believe you," I said as I kissed him on the cheek. "I am going to go by Cynthia's, so we can talk. And I am going to tell her about Jayson. I will drive the Camaro, so don't wait up for me," I said as I left.

37
Confessions

When I arrived at Cynthia's house, her front door was wide open. I looked around, and I didn't see any sign of Daddy.

"Hello!" I shouted from the living room. "Cynthia! Princess! Is anyone home?"

I closed and locked the door behind me. I heard someone sniffing as I walked down the foyer to the family room.

"Cynthia, why is your door wide open? Are you okay?"

She was at the table crying, looking at her wedding pictures.

"It's all my fault," she kept saying repeatedly as she turned up a bottle of Cîroc vodka. "What are you doing here?" she asked as she looked over at me. "I see you're still looking like a woman, but you're all man. That dress that you have on doesn't make you a damn woman. And those fake-ass breasts and that booty pad are a waste."

She said things that got me heated and that got under my skin, but I kept my cool and looked at her and said, "Well, for starters, you are my sister, and I came to check on you. I want us to go and see Mama together. I, also, have some information about Jayson."

"Don't you dare let his name come out of your mouth, you fucking faggot!"

"Why the hostility?" I asked as I sat next to her. "We

were just cool, and now this?"

She was drunk, and I could tell, but I wanted us to put the past behind us.

"I know all about you coming onto Jayson in high school. I know all about Jayson being on the down low. He was fucking your teacher," she screamed. "And he's dead all because of me!" She cried louder and louder. "I know all about him sleeping around with your faggot-ass teacher. All I asked was for Daddy to give me the scoop on Jayson. I didn't know that he would fucking kill him! I had a feeling that he was cheating on me, but never in a million years did I think that it would be a fucking man!"

I knew that she was hurting, so I held her as she continued to cry.

"Why didn't Mama just abort me?" she asked as she grabbed onto me.

"Cynthia, you are drunk, and this vodka is making you say crazy things. I'm not crazy, and I knew that Daddy was going to kill Mama, too. Wait a damn minute! You knew about that and didn't tell anyone?"

"No, I didn't tell anyone because you were always her favorite. *Let Trey have this…and let Trey have that! Trey is a lover not a fighter.* She used to punish me when it was you who was playing in her make-up. She never loved me, just like Daddy never loved you. And I have always despised her for that. So, I guess that makes me an accessory, and I will be going to jail, too. Don't look surprised," she said as she wiped her tears. "You know that I was always the one getting my ass beat because your punk ass wanted to be a girl."

"But, Cynthia, we're family, and that's what blood does."

"Does blood try to fuck my man?"

"That was a long time ago. I didn't know that you guys were going to get married. I was damn near a kid."

"But you knew that you liked boys, and you tried to fuck Jayson."

"You knew that I had been in love with him since grade school."

"I was going to make Daddy's wish come true by helping him get to you."

"Was that what you really wanted?" I said as I began to cry. "You want me dead, too. This has got to stop! If I die, it won't change the fact that Jayson is dead. I came over here because I wanted for us to go see Mama together. If you want me dead that bad, then call Daddy right now because I am tired of running. I have been running for almost three years now. So, if my death will make you happy, then go right ahead and call the sick son of a bitch!"

Then, she looked at me and said, "Trey, I am so mad and hurt at Daddy, and I am taking it out on you. I wish that I had never asked him to follow Jayson. I didn't know that he would kill him. I didn't want Mama to get hurt either, but Daddy sounded so convincing. Trey, I have a confession to make," she said as she went to her bedroom to retrieve a shoe box. "Do these look familiar?" she asked as she pulled out those mystery letters.

"They most certainly do," I said, relieved to know that they were from her and not some random, crazy chick. "Cynthia, but why?" I asked as I looked at the numerous letters. "Oh, my God! You followed me to Miami, too?"

"Yes, I followed you because you were living the life that I used to live. Jayson used to take me out and hold my hand until he started sleeping with your damn teacher. Trey, what do you expect. You were born with hair down your back? You have Mama's big, perky eyes. You have her skin complexion. Hell! You look just like Mama! And look at me! I was the tom boy that got Daddy's looks. I'm sorry for all of these crazy-ass letters, but I really wanted to break up you and Frank. I wanted you to think that he was married with children. That was why I said all of those crazy things. Your man is so faithful and in love with you. One night, I saw him at a club downtown, and I had arranged for this guy to come on to him, but he didn't give him the time of day. You have a good man. Do you know how many bitches would kill to have a man like yours? You are one lucky gal," she said as she pinched my cheek. "Trey, I am so bitter right now, and I blame Mama and Daddy. I blame Mama for not loving me, and I blame Daddy for killing Jayson. Jayson's parents didn't even let me come to his funeral. Even though he was burnt to a crisp, he was still my husband. I don't want to live anymore."

She threw the vodka bottle across the room.

"Whoa! You are really talking crazy right now. We can get through this together."

"But I'm going to go to jail for knowing all about Daddy's plot to kill you and Mama."

"That can stay between just the two of us. I know you're not stupid enough to tell on yourself, are you?"

"Trey, I am scared. I don't want to go to jail, and I don't want you to die. I am so sorry, Trey. Can you please forgive me?"

"Yes, I forgive you, and I love you. We have to stick together and take care of Mama."

"Trey, I have another confession to make. I don't have HIV. I said that to make you feel sorry for me."

"Wow!" I said as I looked at her. "You didn't have to go there. That is something serious, and you're playing about that. You wrote that letter to yourself?"

"I'm sorry for breaking your window. I followed him one night. That's how I know where you guys stay."

I was standing there, looking at Cynthia, thinking that Daddy wasn't the only one losing his mind. She was losing her mind, too.

"Trey, I am so sorry I got caught up in the moment. I wanted it to be all about me, when, in fact, it should be all about you. I know how you feel deep down inside, and I should respect that. Trey, can you stay here with me tonight, so we can go see Mama in the morning? I am such a mess right now, and I smell like a walking alcoholic."

She was right. She couldn't go to the hospital in the shape that she was in. I was hesitant about staying the night with her, but I did anyway.

38
Up All Night

If Cynthia thought I was going to fall asleep in her house, she had another thing coming. I called Frank to let him know that I would be staying with Cynthia for the night. For some strange reason, I wasn't scared anymore. If I was going to die by the hands of my daddy, then so be it, but that didn't change the fact that Cynthia had written all of those crazy-ass letters. How could she joke about having HIV when people die from that disease every day? She definitely had Daddy's ways, but she couldn't help what kind of blood ran through her veins.

After I helped her to her bedroom, she just fell out on the bed. Princess jumped on the bed with her and licked her face. She was drunk as hell, and I didn't see how she was still breathing, considering she had went through three bottles of vodka. I looked around her house, and it was a mess. She had new clothes and shoes everywhere.

"She hasn't even worn most of this stuff yet," I said as I looked at a pair of Rainbow Bottoms. "I see she likes my drag swag, while she's always saying that she hates faggots, yet instead she has Rainbow Bottoms throughout her house."

She was my sister, but it was still hard for me to trust her. She had Daddy's blood flowing through her veins, and neither of them gave a flying fuck about me. I was not about to go to sleep, so I decided to ramble through her shoe box and read her twisted as notes. How could she do such a sick thing to herself? I found a ton of unopened envelopes addressed to me. *This bitch is crazy as hell,* I thought as I scanned through the letters.

"Hmmm… this one is called 'Oil and Water'."

Oil and Water

Everyone knows that oil and water don't mix,
But I promise my relationship with my brother I will fix.
The world is already corrupt and bad as it is,
But all we have to do is keep in touch and continue to live.
Despite of all the shit that we've been through,
We should have each other's back like a crew.
I love my brother, even though he wants to be a damn girl.
And I know that Daddy would never let him live in peace in this world.
I love Trey until this day,
But, when we see each other, we only have sassy words to say.
Speaking like we have some sense will help us so much,
But we hardly ever keep in touch.
Mama wasn't there for the both of us,
And, when she was there for me, it was a big fuss.
One day, we will get it together and perhaps we could be nice,
But I don't think that has a chance in hell, even if we rolled a dice.
I never saw myself actually hating Trey,
But he's the one who made me this way.
He wanted to be a girl so damn bad,
And my man, he just wanted to have.
I thought that all of these crazy letters would make him see
That a real man is what he should be.
How could he even think to get fucked in the ass?
When Jayson tried that shit, I would pass.
I should have known something was wrong then,
But I didn't know where to begin.

I thought that he loved me for me,
But all things aren't what they seemed to be,
And then that faggot-ass teacher came along
And broke up our happy home.

I felt so sad for Cynthia, especially since she'd lost the love of her life, but I had nothing to do with him turning out gay. Hell, I didn't even get a chance to fuck him, so I didn't know why she hated me so much. She needed to just move on and put Jayson behind her. I looked on and read another letter that was addressed to someone named Kelly. It was called "You Ain't No Friend".

I thought that you were my friend and you wanted to see me get ahead,
But I was wrong because you treated me like bread.
I saw the evil and hate in your eyes,
But I came out on top to your surprise.
I helped you with your kids and watched them grow.
Now that I am getting a little fame, you act like you don't know.
You have to understand that I had a dream, and I followed it,
But there is enough money in this world for us both to get.
I found my passion in life and ran with it.
Now you need to find yours and quit hating and shit.
All you want to do is sit outside in the hood,
And you not wanting to get out of the ghetto is something that I've never understood.
If I made it out, then you can, too,
But, girlfriend, your life is entirely up to you.
I was your friend, but you wasn't mine,
But I forgave you and gave you some time
Because you see my heart is good, could never hate,
And now you see that talking about me behind my back was a big

mistake.
I even gave you the keys to my ride.
You went to my house and in my bedroom you tried to hide.
Yeah, my man told me that you came to our home.
While you were on your way, you had me on the phone.
You knew my whereabouts like my time and my place,
But I had a good man who didn't want you all up in his face.
Yes, bitch, there are still a few good men left,
And you're so desperate, he told me that you tried to get him drunk
with the Vodka on the shelf.
Girlfriend, I must say that you have a lot of nerves.
Yeah, stay in the ghetto, bitch, because that's what your ass deserves!

     Damn! She had had a friend who betrayed her, too. I felt so bad for her. I had to do something that would help her and lift her spirits. I was getting sleepy and tired of reading her bullshit. Then, I looked and saw some more interesting letters. Even though her letters were indirect and meaningless, they were simply her feelings put down on paper, and she was a good writer. Instead of being an accountant, she should have been a journalist. I ran across a letter that was called "Not a Happy Ending".

Not a happy ending
And I knew from the beginning.
We were a mix match,
Like a pair of jeans missing a patch.
When we first met, everything was cool.
I'm tired of sitting back being the fool.
They say in this life that you live and learn.
I'm just glad that it's finally my turn.
With the next man, I won't make the same mistakes.

Sleeping with you, countless orgasms I had to fake.
I kept myself up to par.
Some nights, when you would come home, you wouldn't even touch
me after leaving the bar.
You said leave you alone, and you needed some time to think.
Meanwhile, I was feeling like a battleship about to sink.
I feel good, and I feel much better,
Especially when I read your letter.
You wanted me to stay with you and not leave.
You should have thought of that before you made my heart grieve
I knew that you were gay, and I continued to stay
Because you wanted your parents to keep giving you that heavy
pay,
So now I will move on and never look back
You can't break me; I got nine lives, just like a cat.
Daddy told me to stop worrying, that things would be okay,
And he would still be with Mama until this day,
If it wasn't for her faggot-ass son,
Who wants a dick between his bun.
Daddy is from the old school,
And he don't play that gay shit. It's just isn't cool.

I went on to read another one called *"Bitter Bitches"*

There are too many Bitter Bitches roaming the earth.
I believe that their mamas were bitter when they gave birth.
You'll survive. "Just keep living" is the motto that I live by.
Trying to be a Bitter Bitch's friend, I will never try.
They come to work, looking and acting all rude,
When the number one thing they should check is their attitude.
We all have problems and that's nothing new,
But keep all that bullshit away from me, keep it with you.

You're already ugly with that mug on your face.
This is not the time, nor the fucking place.
I come to work to do my fucking job.
You're not going to spoil my day, neither will I sob.
Trying to turn the other cheek, I have already tried,
So I will just ignore the Bitter Bitch, jump in my 745 and ride.

How could I make amends with Cynthia when it was obvious that she was holding grudges against me? She was always flipping on me. One minute, she loved me, and the next minute, she didn't. I couldn't win for losing. I mean, I wanted her in my life, but if she was going to keep downing me, I would have to exclude her from my life.

39
Daddy in the Flesh

I was getting sleepy, and I pissed off at the same time at Cynthia's fucked up letters, but I was so scared to go to sleep in her house especially since she and Daddy kept in contact. I instant messaged Frank on his cell phone, telling him that I loved him and that I would be home the following day. I went to check on Cynthia and found she wasn't in her bed.

Where could she be? I thought as I searched for her throughout her house.

"Cynthia!" I screamed, but there was no answer.

This bitch had better not be up to any trickery, or we're all going to die tonight, I thought. I knew that I should have gone with my first mind and left anyway. I should have known that I couldn't trust her. I wasn't feeling staying there with her after she confessed that it was her that was sending me all those crazy letters anyway. I called Princess, and she didn't even answer.

"This shit isn't funny, Cynthia! Wherever you are, answer me!"

As I walked down to the opposite hall where her bedroom was, I entered a room that was cold, and the walls were covered with photographs of us at all different ages, but my face was blacked out of the pictures.

"I remember this picture," I said as I felt Mama's face.

We had taken a family portrait downtown at Harry's Photography. Even Daddy looked happy in the picture, but I was on there with a black face, and she had colored my teeth green. There were so many different memories coming back to me. She had all of our pictures from elementary school all the way to high school. She had the word *die* written on my forehead on numerous of pictures. I felt uncomfortable. A sense of fear came over me. I felt like I was about to pass out. For some strange reason, I felt evil in that room. Then, all of a sudden, Cynthia appeared out of the closet. She didn't look drunk anymore. There was something definitely different about her. She had on all black. She even had on black gloves.

"What the fuck is going on, Cynthia? And why are you dressed in all black?"

"Trey, let's just get this over with quick," she said as she pulled her hair back into a ponytail.

"Get what over with quick?" I said as I looked around.

"Well, as you can tell, I hate your fucking guts," she said as she looked at the pictures on the wall. I said all of that shit for you to stay here. I wasn't drunk. That was water in that damn Vodka bottle. You always did fall for anything. And now your stupid faggot-ass has fallen in this trap, so Daddy can get your punk ass. It's only right that you die like Jayson did. I was right there when Daddy strangled Jayson. Hell! I held his white ass down. I really wished that Mama would have died, too. She didn't care for me, so why should I care for her? She never loved me, so why should I love her? Trey, women shouldn't have kids if they don't love them. How do you think I felt growing up? You witnessed her whooping me for you playing in her makeup and heels. She was in denial, but she didn't have to take it out on me.

"And you witnessed Daddy beating me," I shouted back.

"He was only trying to beat the gay out of your ass. He didn't want his one and only son to get fucked in the ass and cross-dress like a damn woman. Look at how ridiculous you look in that dress."

"So, this is it, Cynthia? You want my life to end right here in your house?"

"Why not?" Daddy said that it has to be done."

"Cynthia, no! It doesn't have to be done. Daddy has brainwashed you. If Jayson wanted to be gay, you could have bounced back from that. Cynthia, homosexuality doesn't stop with me. Half of the world is fucking gay. Plus, I am your brother. Doesn't that mean anything to you? Think about it, Cynthia. Once I am dead, then what?"

"Trey, Daddy says that you have to die," she said as she hit herself upside her head.

"Cynthia, it's me. Trey," I said as I took off of the fake breasts and the butt pads. "There! Are you happy now?"

I snatched my eyelashes off one by one. I wiped my rose pink lip gloss off and walked over to her.

"Cynthia, I promise you will never see me again. Cynthia, please let me go before Daddy gets here."

"I'm already here, you punk motherfucker," I heard Daddy's voice say.

40
My Father's Seed

I turned around and looked Daddy dead in his eyes. I hadn't seen him in such a long time. I shook like a leaf with the butt pad in my hand.

"No need to be afraid now. You wasn't afraid when you were out there sucking dicks and getting fucked in your ass. Trey, how many times did I tell you that I brought you in this world and I will take your punk ass out!"

"Plenty of times, Daddy," I said as I swallowed hard.

Cynthia just stood there, looking like she was ready for some action. I was shit out of luck. *God, this cannot be happening,* I thought as I prayed silently. Daddy had a look on his face that I would never forget. He had an army fatigue bandana around his bald head, and he had black make up under his eyes. He looked like he was ready to go to war, not kill his son.

My heart was beating at about one thousand beats per minute. My hands were sweating profusely, and I felt like I was about to faint. I wished that I had at least had on regular clothes and not a dress. Daddy was looking at me like I was making him sick to his stomach, but, in reality, he was making me sick to mine. I literally felt knots in my stomach. I felt very anxious, and I had nowhere to run. I never imagined my life being like this in a million years. If Daddy kills me for being gay, someone was going to make a movie about it. This was just absurd.

Then, I had a flashback. We were all eating dinner at

the table. It was the four of us, and we were such a happy family back then. Daddy had cooked curry chicken, black beans, and spicy cabbage with mixed vegetables. It was sad to say, but food was the only thing that brought us together as a family. Usually, I was getting my ass beat by Daddy because I didn't catch a damn football or because I had skipped football practice. Or Cynthia would be getting her ass beat by Mama because I was playing in her makeup. So now I understood why Cynthia was so mad with Mama. Mama had been in such denial that she would actually see her red lipstick on my lips and still whoop Cynthia. She would scream at Cynthia and say that she should not have let me go in her room, but the only one who could stop me from going in there was Daddy, and he was always at the fire station.

I snapped back to reality, and, as soon as I tried to run past Daddy, he grabbed me by my throat and tried to choke the life out of me. I tried to get his hands from around my neck, but Daddy was too strong. I felt my finger bleed as the fake nails broke off one by one. I looked over at Cynthia as I tried to gasp for air, but it was useless because she was egging Daddy on.

She said, "Die like the rest of those faggots! Kill him, Daddy, just like you killed Jayson. He doesn't deserve to live."

I looked into Daddy's eyes and saw nothing but hatred. He was so cold, and I couldn't break his grip from around my neck for nothing. I remembered that Cynthia had told me that Daddy could kill with his bare hands.

Daddy said, "You don't deserve to live. No son of mine will be acting like a damn girl. And you have the nerve to have this fucking dress on. I have been waiting a long time for this. I have been patiently waiting to choke the shit out of you. If you want something done, you have to do it yourself. And this is such a pleasure to finally drain the life out of you slowly."

As I started to see nothing but black, I saw Mama, and she said, "Don't be afraid. God has his hands over you."

I was starting to see my life flash before my eyes. I saw my high school graduation... I saw Big Steve punch me in my stomach... I saw myself on the stage at Club Same Attraction... I had on an eye-catching black and ivory cocktail dress with plenty of flares... My hair was spiraled all the way down my back...My smoky eyes were to die for with a long pair of eyelashes. The eyelashes cornered the edge of my eyes, which made me look super hot. I had on a black pair of Chris's Rainbow Bottoms. I was on stage looking my best. I eyed the crowd and sang the song "Nowhere to Run" by Martha and the Vandellas. Frank and Mama were right there on the front row, clapping their hands to the beat. Everyone was enjoying me singing my heart out. Then, all of a sudden the crowd began to say my name repeatedly, "Trey! Trey! Trey! Trey!"

I opened my eyes, and it was Frank.

41
Free at Last

I was lying on my back, and Frank was screaming my name.

"Am I dead? Where am I? Where's Daddy?"

"I'm here for you, and your daddy and Cynthia are locked up. That's just where they belong. We're still at Cynthia's house. There are policemen and detectives all over this place. We have it all on tape, so you can stop running and live your life. On the day when I came over here with you to visit her, I crept back into this room and placed this tiny camera on the wall. I had a funny feeling about her, and you told me about how much she hated you, so I was ten steps ahead of them. My plan was to kill two birds with one stone and that was exactly what I did. I have them both on video, and that's all the evidence that the police need to put them both away in jail for good. When I talked to you last night, and, when you told me that you were going to spend the night here at Cynthia's, I didn't think that it was a good idea, so that's how my plan came into play. I didn't want to say anything to frighten you because I already knew that your daddy was hiding in the house. I drove over here and waited. I saw you two through the window. I watched as you consoled her and cried with her. I told you that I love you and I would never let anything happen to you, but it also looks like God was on our side, too, because, when you pointed at this picture of you all, the camera cut off. The police and I ran in here just in a nick of time. Your daddy was five seconds away from strangling you to death. You have a big red bruise around your neck, but that will heal in a couple of days. My main concern is that you still have air in our lungs."

I was still in a daze. I thought that I was dead. As I laid there in Frank's arms, I finally moved my mouth and said, "The last thing I remember is singing 'Nowhere To Run' on stage, and you and Mama were right in the front row."

He interrupted me and said, "Speaking of Mama, she's out of the coma, and she will be coming home soon."

"So now I am finally free," I said as I felt my neck. "Now, things can go back to normal. I am finally free at last. I no longer have to run from that crazy-ass man. I can live like a normal drag queen. I can live without getting hassled by my own damn family."

I looked around Cynthia's room, and I started to take our pictures down one by one.

"I don't know what came over her. It's like she was possessed by Daddy and the devil," I said as I snatched the pictures aggressively.

"I have gathered all of your things," Frank said as he showed me my butt pad and detachable breasts.

"Thanks," I said as I smiled at him.

He was really a great guy, and I couldn't ask God for a better mate. I walked past him and grabbed my attachments. I headed to Cynthia's bathroom to put them back on. She even had pictures of me in there with the word DIE written across my forehead. She needed to be in a mental ward because she was mentally ill.

"Let's go," I said as I stood there looking at him. He was standing there looking like the hero that he was. "Let's go see Mama," I said as I grabbed his hand and headed out the door.

I locked up her house as we left. As I was about to

get in our car, I looked over at a squad car and saw Daddy. Even though he couldn't get to me, I was still terrified. He looked as if he was going away on vacation. He was looking straight ahead. Cynthia, on the other hand, was screaming, jumping up and down. She was saying that she was sorry and that it was all Daddy's fault.

"That's what you get, bitch," I said as I got in the car with Frank.

Our ride was long and silent. I didn't want to talk about Daddy or Cynthia. All I wanted to do was see Mama. I was going to give her the biggest, warmest hug that I could ever give her. I was glad to know that she was out of the coma and doing alright. She was all that I had left, and I was going to make sure that Frank and I took really good care of her.

I had just remembered the two letters that I had grabbed from Cynthia's bathroom and decided to read them. One of them was called "The Mistress".

I will be here for your man. Yes, your man,
So, if you want to keep him, you better come up with a better plan.
You need to listen to him and do the things that he likes
Because he usually ends up in my bed after you all had a fight.
He does weird shit, like call me your name when we're having sex,
But I don't care. He bought me a house, so there's no telling what's next.
He confided in me and told me that shit that you two go through,
So you can't blame no one for his cheating, but you.
I didn't want a man of my own.
All I wanted to do was fuck them and send them back home.
Your husband is so nice to me. He's never mean,
And guess what? We've been fucking since he was sixteen.
He talks to me about how you never took dick in the ass,

But that's my favorite, and I will never pass.
You better woman up and get with the program
And stop stuffing your face with all that damn ham.
He tells me that you're fat and out of shape.
He also said that you're starting to look like an fat ass ape.
These are his own words coming out of his mouth,
But I heard that men like Big Girls down south.
I know what your man wants, believe me. I understand
Because I am not a woman. I AM A MAN!!!

Wow! That one sounded like that it was from Ronnie. He had some fucking nerves, but hell! What could I do about it? It was none of my business. That was strictly between Jayson, Cynthia and Ronnie. No wonder Cynthia was so pissed at Ronnie. He has been sending her letters, too. This was some crazy shit. She was in a love triangle, but none of the corners had anything to do with her. I went on to read the other one that was called "The Unhappy Wife".

All those unhappy years that I spent
You tried not to leave me one red cent.
I was a good wife and I held on.
I even stayed strong on those nights when you didn't come home.
He was a good man when I said, "I do."
And I believed when you said that "I love you."
But no one should have to wear my shoes not even me.
Never in a millions years did I pictured this for my life to be
I never had the strength to leave
But not only was I wrapped around your pinky, I was also wrapped around your sleeve,
So I swallowed the fact that you was cheating with a man whore.
I even thought about cheating to even the score
I was a faithful, loving and caring wife,

So that's why I had arranged for daddy to end your life.

42
Mama's Coming Home

After I finished reading Cynthia's fucked up letters, I shredded them to pieces. We arrived at the hospital, and I was so happy to go in and see Mama. It had been almost five years since I had last seen her. We arrived inside the hospital, and, once again, all eyes were on me as I walked to the information booth.

"I'm looking for Mrs. Carolyn Burns," I said as I twirled my hair.

"She's on the fifth floor," she said, looking at me up and down.

"Thanks," I said as I walked off with an attitude.

It didn't matter what I had on. I would always get some of the dirtiest stares from people. I got on the elevator and headed to the fifth floor. Frank stayed in the car. He said that he wanted my moment to be special with Mama, so he didn't mind waiting in the car. My heart started beating rapidly the closer I got to Mama's room. I peeked in. She was sitting up, watching *Sanford and Son*.

"You always liked that show," I said as I walked in.

"Trey? Is that you?" she said as she turned the television off.

"Yes, it's me, Mama," I said as I sat next to her on the bed. "Can I hug you? Aren't you fragile?" I said as tears came to my eyes.

"Boy, you better get over here and give your mama a hug."

We hugged each other, and I didn't want to let her go. She started to cry. Then, she looked at me and said, "Have you had that operation?"

"No, I didn't, and I'm not even sure if I am going to go through with it. These are detachable," I said as I looked around the room, noticing all the colorful balloons. "I have a lot to tell you. Daddy and Cynthia are in jail."

"They found him?" Mama said as tears started to fall down her face again. "I remember that day like yesterday, when he came to Barbara's place. He was so furious, and, as I tried to reason with him and calm him, it was too late. The next thing that I knew, I was in the hospital, but these doctors here at Grady are so good. They saved my life, and the nurses have been so nice to me. I could have been out of this place, but since Daddy was on the run, I had around the clock security. Step back and let me look at you."

She wiped her tears.

"It's me. I am the same old Trey," I said as I sort of tilted the bottom of my dress. I knew that Mama wasn't all that excited to see her son standing there in a dress, but she really didn't have a choice. This is what I want to do so this is what I'm going to do. We gathered her things and headed to the car. Frank was already in the front waiting on us. She looked as if she wanted to see Ronnie or Chris. Frank got out and opened up the door for her.

He said, "I am glad to finally meet you."

He closed the door, and I sat in the back seat.

She said, "I am glad to meet you, too, and to finally see my son."

"Mama, this is my man Frank, and he's been there for me since day one."

"I just want to get somewhere and relax. Being in that hospital has really drained me," Mama said as she strapped in her seatbelt.

"Don't worry, Mama. We're going to my place, and it will soon be your place. It's comfy, and I even have that country kitchen that you always dreamed of."

I knew that Mama was probably still distraught because her own husband and daughter tried to kill her, but I was going to make her as comfortable as possible. I could tell that she wasn't too fond of seeing me in a dress. I felt some type of way when she first seen me. I sat back and began to write in my diary.

Dear Diary,

I am so glad that Mama and I are back together again. She has been through so much these last few years. And all I want to do is be there for her as a son or maybe even a daughter. I hate looking at that huge scar around her neck, knowing that Daddy did it all because of me. She's still pretty though. She still has her unending beauty. However, I am still so confused as to whether I want to have this surgery or not. Mama and I will have a heart to heart conversation about it. I know that my surgery is the last thing that she wants to talk about considering all that she has been through. But she has told me over and over that she's here for me and she will support anything that I do. I can't help but weep for Mama deep down in my heart. She was so helpless and all she knew was love. Hell! She's the reason why I am so quick to forgive. She always assured me that I shouldn't fight fire with fire when I was younger. She'd always say, "Trey, just turn the other cheek and ignore those kids who make fun of you." Well, I turned the other cheek alright, and it was my ass cheek. But, in all seriousness, I love my mama to death, and I am so glad that she didn't die. If she would have died, I don't know what I would have done without her. She's my rock, my best friend and, most importantly, she's my mama. My only mama! I wouldn't trade her for nothing in the world.

43
Home Sweet Home

As time went on, Mama and I became even closer. She had grown accustomed to my relationship with Frank. Frank thought that it would only be fair if he'd given her some of her money back. But Mama insisted that we keep it because she had renter's insurance on our house. She didn't want to move by herself, so I made my whole downstairs hers. She didn't want to live alone after what happened to her. And I didn't want her to live alone either. Daddy's crazy ass would probably break out of jail just to get to us again. I was glad when the judge had given him twenty-five years for what he had done. But he should have gotten life after all that he had done.

It was so hard for Mama to point Daddy out in court. She was in tears as the defense lawyer asked her to point Daddy out.

Cynthia didn't get much time as daddy did because she pleaded mentally ill. It turns out that she was schizophrenia. She was supposed to have been taking medication, and she was prescribed a therapist, but she ignored all of her psychological business and helped Daddy instead. She had a good lawyer, and he got her charges dropped from attempted murder to insanity. Mama wasn't ready to face her and I wasn't either. Mama said that she knew that Cynthia was seeing a therapist, but she didn't know how ill she was. At times, she even blamed herself for everything that happened. She said that she shouldn't have punished Cynthia for my actions as a child. She said, when she built her nerves up, that she would go and visit her.

She was in a mental institution down south. She had to live in a psychiatric hospital for a minimum of five years. That served that bitch correctly. She should be doing hard time like Daddy.

I didn't hear much from Chris and Ronnie, but I did hear that Chris moved to Miami. I was just glad to put the past behind me. Frank, Mama and I lived like one big happy family. She didn't want to bring up the past, and I didn't either. Instead, we pampered ourselves and went shopping and did a lot of girlie stuff together. We often shopped until we dropped. Mama bought herself a 2012 Mercedes Benz C-Class coupe. For the most part, Mama had accepted the dresses, long lashes and stilettos that I rocked. She didn't say too much about my fake body parts either. There would be some days that she would help me get dressed.

She didn't pressure me about the surgery, and I hadn't quite made up my mind. I was comfortable with dressing like a woman. And, besides, Frank really didn't want me to have the surgery because he loved when we made love. He loved to moan my name and I loved to scream his. It didn't matter how many times he lubed his dick up and fucked me in my ass, I could never get used to it. But we loved each other and that was pretty much all that mattered. Mama called Auntie Barbara and she came by to visit mama. She didn't care for me and I still didn't like her ass either.

She had the nerve to bring her ass over to our house with all those disobedient ass kids. Chiquita, her oldest daughter, was still outspoken, but what can I say? She was my little smart ass cousin, and she wasn't used to seeing me dolled up. But Auntie Barbara was mama's sister, and she was all that she had left. Kym was still locked up and had about seven more years to go. I wrote her from time to time but I could never bring myself to go visit her in prison. There was just something about those jail cells that scared me. She wrote back and told me that she learned her lesson and she also said that she wanted to tell me that she saw Cynthia in Miami. But Cynthia told her don't tell me because she wanted to surprise me. But that wasn't a damn surprise. It was one of her stalking ass letters. I never had the chance to confront Ronnie for fucking Jayson. But I didn't want him to confront me for fucking Chris. So I accepted that what was already done was done. I had my mama back and I had a good man. There was nothing more that I could ask for.

Frank and I never really spoke about getting married. We knew that we both had never-ending love for one another. And I really didn't see the point for us to get married. He had my back and I had his back. We still went to Club Same Attraction from time to time. He would enjoy watching me dress in drag and sing to him. He always sat on the front row and I would use him as my focus point. Mama came on a few occasions and she was proud that I was finally living my dream. But one night after a show and just when I thought that shit couldn't get any worse. We returned home to find Trish on our door steps.

"I have been looking for you for a long time. Seven years to be exact," Trish shouted. "And what the fuck do you have on?" she said as she looked me up and down. "Are you fucking gay? I knew I shouldn't have ever fucked you. Are you a fucking drag queen?'

Frank and Mama were speechless, and so was I, when Trish told me that she had my seven-year-old son, waiting in the car.

About The Author

Antoinette Tunique Smith was born in San Francisco, California and raised in ATL, where she still resides. She is blessed with five children who are known as the five lights of her life: Pinky, Driah, Clyde, Chicken and Fat Boy.

She would like people to know that it doesn't matter where you come from, you can be whatever you wanna be. Just believe in God. There is a God!

Thanks &
Much respect,
Antoinette Smith

AND PLEASE CHECK OUT ANTOINETTE'S
PREVIOUSLY RELEASED BOOKS:

*DADDY'S FAVORITE POP
*MARRIED: SNEAKY BLACK WOMAN
*WHITE COP, LIL' BLACK GURL

AND PLEASE STAY TUNED FOR ANTOINETTE'S
UPCOMING BOOKS:

BLACK-OUT ON BANKHEAD
WOMEN R DOGS TOO!
I'M BI WHY LIE?
TREY AND HIS DNA (SEQUEL TO *I'M A DRAG, NOT A FAG*)
I WISH I WAS RAISED (MY LIFE'S STORY)
MY FATHER'S SEED (SEQUEL TO *DADDY'S FAVORITE POP*)
MARRIED, SNEAKY BLACK MAN (SEQUEL TO *MARRIED, SNEAKY BLACK WOMAN*)

I really hope you guys enjoy my Straight to the Point Books!!

Reader Comments from straighttothepontbooks.com:

Tonya – Atlanta, Ga. - 2/28/12
Daddy's Favorite Pop WOW! What a great read. I started to read the book at 4pm and was done by 10pm… I think that so many young girls can relate, benefit and learn from this book! Growing up somewhat of the same kind of environment, it touches basis on everything that can help our young girls and boys from going down the wrong path in life and understanding that they are not alone! It's a perfect example of how NOT TO JUDGE A BOOK BY IT'S COVER and behind that every face, it really is a story to tell. I'm an avid reader and inspiring writer myself and I recommend this book to anyone. It's a great read! Promise you won't put it down!

M. Wylie - Holly Springs N.C - 5/18/10
I was in Atlanta visiting family and we stopped at Greenbriar Mall. My husband and I noticed Medu bookstore , but we were stopped by Antoinette regarding her book "Daddy's Favorite Pop". I LOVE to read African-American novels and support our literary up and coming, so without hesitation, I bought the book. I started reading it about 3pm on Saturday (05/15/10). Let's just say that I was so moved by the story that I finished the book around 2am that morning! This was a well written book and very different from my normal reads. I guess it was the fact that this was someone's life. There were times that the rawness of it all was a bit uncomfortable, but I walked away honored that Antoinette chose to share her story with me. I am definitely a new follower and can't wait to read your other works! You have a literary gift that you should continue to share with the world. Good Luck and Blessings to you.

Gwendolyn - Gainesville Ga. - 5/3/10
Heard you on V-103 last week with my 16 year old daughter in the car with me – we both were in tears by the time you finished telling

your story — — ordered book, received book it in the mail today. — started and finished it — couldn't put it down.... You are Blessed and Highly Favored of God — only he could have gotten you through all that you went through... Trying to decide if I should let my daughter read it... It was tough for me so maybe I will wait a few years before I let her read it... I have suggested it to my friends as a must read... God Bless

Kelly Pugh - Dalton Ga. - 5/4/10

This was a hard read. I couldn't see through the tears. So many times we're on the outside and think we know but have no idea what goes on behind the INFAMOUS closed doors. Continue to be Blessed!!!

Andrea Bell - Hampton Ga. - 3/15/10

OMG... I had the pleasure of meeting Ms. Smith today and she is a wonderful woman!! I purchased "Daddy's Favorite Pop" while at a restaurant and wasn't able to put it down until I read the novel and its entirety!! That says a lot considering I haven't picked up a book that I was interested in enough to read it in a day in years!!! Ms. Smith you are truly an inspiration, PLEASE continue the EXCELLENT work!! I definitely look forward to reading all of your novels and poetry!

LaChrisha - Greeneville S.C. - 3/31/11

I thoroughly read both "Daddy's Favorite Pop" and "Married,Sneaky Black Woman". I love a book that gets me so engrossed in the characters and the storyline and I CAN"T put it down(lol). I read both books within a day literally. Definite page turners and very well written. At the end of "Daddy's Favorite Pop" I kind of felt rushed like the story had run its course,wrapped up, and ended fairly quickly. I was like "awl man" but Married, Sneaky Black Woman I felt complete. I wish you the best of luck with your future endeavors. I pray for your continued success and favor.=)

P.S My Boo done started reading them now(lol)

Kea Neavah - College Park, Ga. - 6/22/11

I have been a fan since Daddy's fav pop! I put all my friends on ur book and I have just finished ur second novel "Married,Sneaky Black Woman"....bravo!!! Ur creativeness and imagination mixed with the truth has inspired me to continue to write my novel about my life. I'm actually a songwriter with Sesac.... but I've always wanted to put out my book and U r now my favorite author! I C U around and I always be like "Girl there goes my author right there!!" Ima always support ya! Great minds think alike. Congrats on your Success. I also got my mom to read ur books! She is a Big Fan now. =) God Bless

Sheneka Jones - Atlanta Ga. - 1/25/12

I want everybody to know I read these 3 books within 2 weeks. (Daddy's Favorite Pop) (Married, Sneaky Black Woman) (White Cop, Lil Black Gurl) They are Great Books, my husband and mom has read them as well and agree 100%. Ms. Smith is so talented and such a awesome writer. I can't wait for the new book to be released.

Karen Clark - Decatur Ga. - 4/23/10

This book was AWESOME!!! I started reading it about 3 days ago. It was sooo powerful and sooo mind blowing til I had to take a break from reading for a day. The way you (Antoinette) had to grow up and all the pain that you endured growing up I commend you. You started as a small pedal and grew into a BEAUTIFUL and AMAZING WOMAN!!! As always follow your heart. I know one day you will learn how to love your children cause God is good All the TIME!!!

Ruby Rios - Norcross Ga. - 1/31/11

This book was totally awesome! I read the book in one day because once I started it I couldn't put it down. Knowing that it was based on a true story really affected my emotions. I was so angry at so many of the characters! I couldn't stop thinking about the story for days!!! I had the pleasure of meeting you in person at the Ranchero and speaking to you and you are a wonderful person. I wish you ALL the best in the world. You deserve it! Can't wait to read the next one. You have a lifetime fan in me!!!! God bless~

Shamika Lockett - Columbia S.C. - 2/23/11

Ms. Smith I wanted to tell you that i really enjoyed your books I have read both of them (Daddy's Favorite Pop) & (Married, Sneaky Black Woman) and they were excellent......I am looking forward to reading more of your books. You do have a fan... "you go girl"

Latisha - Richmond Va. - 2/7/11

This book was so good from start to finish. It kept me on the edge of my seat with all the plots, twists, and turns. This book Never had a dull moment. I look forward to reading your other books.

Cassaundra a.k.a Cignature Fraze - Atlanta Ga. - 3/16/11

I purchased "Married, Sneaky Black Woman" the day that it was released and read it from cover to cover in less than 6 hours because I could only put it down to quickly grab a snack and return. This book was another good read penned by Antoinette. Looking forward to your next one and I must say.... Antoinette I am so proud of you! Live your dream to the fullest! I'll see you at the top! (From one writer to another)

Aisha - Riverdale Ga. - 5/29/11

I was at a local restaurant (Big daddy's) and there you were. I so love your books, you are such an amazing person. I wish that your books were MOVIES they are so good. Love Aisha.... Can't wait to see you on the BIG SCREEN!!!

Debra Hartwell - 10/10/10

Your books saddens my spirit. I pray for other kids that are going through this same thing. I believe you will be a blessing to someone that has gone through and are afraid to speak up. My prayers go out to you and your family. I'm so glad that God kept you while you went through. Be blessed!

www.straighttothepointbooks.com

acansing2000@yahoo.com

www.ingramcontent.com/pod-product-compliance
Lightning Source LLC
Chambersburg PA
CBHW050353030726
47503CB00006B/1839